Love Rita

Ivan the
Giant

PHILIP A CREURER

Ivan the Giant
Copyright © 2019 by Philip A Creurer

Tellwell Talent
www.tellwell.ca

ISBN
978-0-2288-1398-9 (Hardcover)
978-0-2288-1397-2 (Paperback)
978-0-2288-1399-6 (eBook)

For my first editors:

Jim and Hanna
Sam and Owen

CHAPTER ONE

W hen I was eleven, I grew twelve inches and they called me Ivan the Giant. "Hey, Giant Ivan, reach my book for me!" I wasn't liking it. I would not own it. But I wouldn't say anything about it, either. I was a January child, which meant that I was slightly older than most of my classmates in the grade six class, so maybe my age was partly to blame, if I was looking for something to blame, that is, which I wasn't. Nevertheless, it made me sound like some hairy beast from a nursery rhyme, a curiosity dreamed up to either frighten children or be their secret friend. I wasn't scary and I had no intention of being someone's imaginary friend, to be left behind when childish dreams were boxed up and put away, to be replaced by adult pretense.

My arms and legs grew proportionately, and my hands and feet too. So that was lucky. But I was never quite sure where my arms were, and my legs flayed out dangerously at inconvenient moments. Most boys have their growth spurt a bit later, so I was an exception. Not exceptional, but an exception. There is a difference.

Ivan the Giant. The name would not leave me. Why Ivan? I don't know. Who names their kid Ivan? Especially with a last name like Morrow. Ivan Morrow. It might make some sense if my name was Ivanoff or Rachmaninoff or even Schmakovski. But Ivan Morrow? What kind of parents invent that kind of name? My parents were as unexceptional as their progeny, at least in my mind. Like the parents of all my classmates, they went to work every day. They cooked and cleaned and took me on holiday, which I appreciated. In every way, I thought, they seemed like every other parent of every other child. So how did they decide on such an exceptional name? Parents, I decided, are a mystery. Most of my friends shortened their names to one syllable. Tom not Thomas. Mike not Michael. But what does one do with Ivan? "Iv" doesn't really work. My name would not conform to local custom. I was only ever Ivan. And then Ivan the Giant.

Still, the new name opened up some possibilities. I tried out for basketball and actually got on the team. People overlooked my lack of talent for height. It was my first realization that physical traits sometimes are at the root of success rather than any innate ability or commitment to hard work. The unfairness of life worked to my advantage at eleven. I was happy to take what I could get. I was vaguely aware that I looked like a stick man in basketball shorts and top, but not to the point of self-consciousness. I did not glide across the court. I did not float. I got from one end of the basketball court to the other in a series of premeditated lunges, efficacious rather than elegant. But it got the job done. I knew already that my future did not lie with basketball. I was all right with that.

Unlike many of my peers, I was taller even than the girls in my class who generally dwarfed the boys. So, there was that. But nobody called *them* Catherine the Monster or Big Betsy. Anyway, Betsy wasn't someone you wanted to mess with. Her name didn't at all reflect what she could do to you when her temper flared up. What I did notice was that expectations were different for me. Somehow, I was expected to measure up, so to speak, to a standard of maturity commensurate with my height. That was not possible. I was still eleven. I acted and thought like I was eleven. That was natural, at least to me. But when you step into the role of someone of exception, suddenly you are expected to be exceptional. In such circumstances, one learns to cope with others' disappointment. In such circumstances, one can become morose or one can become a cheerful disappointer. I was cheerful. Most of the time. It helped others get over their disappointment in my rather ordinary level of performance. Part of a healthy life is breaking other people's expectations of oneself.

Math was my thing. I liked the neat way it worked itself out. With black lines on white ruled paper, math told a story. A train is speeding west at sixty kilometres per hour. A car is being driven at seventy kilometres per hour. The car starts an hour late from the train station. How long will it take to catch up to the train? A simple story. A simple solution. There is a beginning and there is an end. Satisfaction. Resolution. Don't bother that the road maybe doesn't run parallel with the train tracks.

I was an only child, which should have given me some kind of complex, like being unusually selfish. But I wasn't particularly self-centred. No more than anyone at eleven, that is. I had been taught by Walter and Macy to share and to play nice with others. I did relish time by myself, if that counts as selfishness. Nor did I have cousins nearby to spend time with. It was just me and Macy and Walter. They left me alone to figure things out by myself in my own time. Not that I was alone. My best friend was Thomas. Tom Andrew. He had two first names. When I first met him, it took a while to remember which was his first and which was his last name. Tom Andrew. Not Thomas Andy. Not Tom Andy. Not Thomas. But Tom. Tom Andrew. He got my name right from the first meeting. Ivan. Who forgets an Ivan? He never called me Ivan the Giant. We met in second grade when he moved to our neighbourhood. He sat in a discreet corner of the classroom trying to be inconspicuous, which was not really possible. I said "Hi" at recess. He said "Hi" back. And so we became friends. Even though he didn't share my interest in math.

Tom's thing was science. He liked the smelly science room with its hamsters churning up woodchips, jars of icky green slime, and posters pinned up crookedly on the wall to remind us of what was beyond the scope of our own experience: space shuttle, space station, sea urchins, and Mars. Invitations to hopeful ambition, urged on by the promise reserved to those, like us, standing on the threshold of a new millennium. Tom's parents were named Alice and Rick. Alice was rather beautiful, with blond hair and easy fashion. Rick was tall, thin, and red. Alice and Rick were substantial. I was slightly in awe. They orbited the adult world in a way my parents never did. My parents were evanescent, changeable. Macy and Walter. Their planet was Earth. But Rick and Alice hailed from a more permanent but inaccessible world, just beyond my reach. Tom negotiated the world of Rick and Alice with ease and familiarity. I felt marooned whenever I was there.

"Hello, Ivan. Nice to see you," Alice would say, and I would counter with cheerful aggression, "Thanks for having me over, Mrs. Andrew. It's always fun here." She would smile and blink for a second before turning around.

Tom and I were friends with Lisa. Lisa Troll. It was an unfortunate name, one of those happenstances in life that must be taken on the chin. But Lisa was not burdened by her name or in any way bothered by it. She suffered no trauma and, in fact, she could, on occasion, make a joke of it. No doubt this disarmed those who sought to taunt her. She radiated a certain self-possession that expressed itself chiefly in a masterful capacity to organize anything or anyone. On the other hand, Tom was the most disorganized person I had ever met, which seemed to contradict his attraction for the natural sciences and their neat classification of all that lives and moves and is. Walking into Tom's bedroom was an adventure into an unclassified world where pillows, scribblers, socks, and fish inhabited one indistinct category of being, clashing in space and competing for precedence. Lisa was the opposite. Her world needed only the discovery of a new species of box or list to make the whole thing orbit around her in an orderly manner. Her charm was her innate sense of order. It was a charm where charm otherwise was absent. She did have nice eyes, though. Clear blue eyes that danced to some unheard-of melody.

One summer night in fourth grade, Tom and I had decided to camp out in my back yard. We thought his parents would be more cooperative than mine in allowing him to stay over. We had colluded with Lisa — Leese — to arrange that she would escape from her house later in the evening and come over and sleep in the tent with us. Tom and I spent the afternoon by a pond in the park, scaring minnows and slapping mosquitoes. We heard a frog and spent an eternity trying to locate the rasping call, which became increasingly annoying the longer our fruitless search endured. Once, on a similar afternoon, we had seen a small turtle sunbathe in the warmth on a stick that lay protruding from the surface of the still water. It stretched its neck in majestic unconcern for the danger around it. We had resisted the temptation to find a twig and prod it from its slumber. But the turtle had abandoned us. Dusk fell and we found our way home as grasshoppers invaded the cooling evening.

We pitched our tent without help. A satisfying accomplishment. Mom brought my sleeping bag with a pillow from somewhere out of storage and Tom and I settled in as night invaded. Tom brought his sleeping bag but had forgotten his pillow. It lay, no doubt, on the floor of his bedroom guarded by watchful fish. We munched on chips, sitting cross-legged and talking about nothing in particular. Stars and moonwalks and trains. Ants ran across our ankles and there was the slight hum of a world's motion about us. I was lazily leaning back when the creak of the fence gate betrayed the arrival of Leese. We had left it slightly open on purpose so that she might steal in. She sat with us and joined our listless conversation. She had brought food, insect repellant, a sleeping bag, and a pillow, all fitted neatly into a small black bag. We discussed whether I should go into the house to ask for another pillow, but we worried it might arouse suspicion. Slowly, we talked ourselves to the sleepy verge of quiet. When we lay down in the tent, Leese and Tom decided to share her pillow. Given the circumstances, it seemed the best solution.

Leese had also grown in the last year. She was not quite as tall as I, but taller than Tom. So together, corporately, we balanced each other out. Her interest lay chiefly in history. Social sciences it was called, a catch-all category that stretched to reach the outer limits of the teacher's knowledge, which mostly came from our textbook. Dates and events were noted on a time chart lining the front wall above the chalkboard. It started with the picture of a dinosaur peeking around a tropical frond and ended with a satellite spinning in a dark sky spotted with twinkling stars. Reaching back and reaching to the present, the future was left white and undefined. In between were interspersed a series of ape-like men, golden pharaohs, crowned kings, and warring soldiers. Women, apparently, were invisible to world history. The ordered, regular progression of dates appealed to Leese. Time made sense of the chaos of the cosmos. She saw herself drawn into the timeline and the onward march of history. The order of it all betokened a purpose. She had an amazing catalogue of facts concealed in her head, and ever-lengthening lists of events. Whereas Tom registered the cause and effect of the natural world, Leese revelled in the volitional abyss of human conduct. It made sense to her. I, on the other hand, was stuck in purely abstract figures, a wayfarer only on the timeline of history and a passive pawn in the great net of life. Until I was eleven, this was experienced unconsciously and not with any sense of revolt. At eleven one can still easily accept one's lot in life, and it is a given that others will prod and pull us through the day. Yet there is the glimmer that all is not as it seems, that a burgeoning power from within will burst forth one day into cataclysmic ordinariness.

I had heard that in high school, students moved from one class to another. There was an enticing anticipation to this stream of nomadic student life. Here, we spent the day within the same walls, except when we had science. In high school, students pitched a mobile camp in the quarters of their teachers; here, we lived a sedentary existence as the teacher shifted from one theme to another and we shifted in our seats. My sixth-grade teacher was nice. Mrs. Phillips. I would have preferred Mr. Maugher. He had a beard and wore a tie, which he pinched repeatedly even though he always left the top button of his shirt open. He reigned over a slightly chaotic domain and had a hunted, harried look in his eyes, as if something had just caught him out and he was coping with the unexpected.

There was no room for the unexpected in Mrs. Phillips' classroom. Chalkboards were clean and unmarked each morning when we entered, white chalk interspersed at convenient intervals in the long, fluted tray lining the bottom of the chalkboard. A package of coloured chalk waited on the corner of the desk, neatly placed beside essential tools of the trade: stapler, pen, one sheet of blank paper, and the fake leather attendance card holder in the upper right corner, folded until needed. Everything else was tucked neatly away in drawers which we never saw opened, but which we imagined contained geometrically colour-coded holders for erasers, highlighters, paperclips, and loose-leaf — "foolscap" she called it. Class subjects were treated in fifty-seven-minute segments, giving us just enough time to put the books of one subject away and find the books for the next; a chance to move and glance out of the windows at the ground around or in the sky above. A swallow in aerial ballet; a squirrel sitting, dashing, and then skirting tree trunks in furtive measures of deception; a dog barking in the distance, invading for a moment the ordered indoor lives necessary to the study of English, Math, Social Sciences, and French. A regulated pause in an ordered unfolding of the morning.

Tom had a quick mind, a wonderful ability to scout out the land and zero in on the essentials, like a spy plane that flies hidden above the clouds to seek out all the detail of the landscape, recording every dreary undulation, searching through the commonplace for the one piece of data that does not fit. I was more interested in the flight than the path. It wearied my brain to seek out what did not belong. I was interested in patterns, not peculiarities. Puzzles only annoyed me.

It was all the more surprising, then, that I was soon to became obsessed with a conundrum that I could not tuck away or ignore. It was a mental puzzle that would not go away and it led me where I would not otherwise have wished to go. It started innocently enough as another unwelcome demand on my precious free time. I was realizing that getting older meant other people thought they had a right to my leisure time.

In mid-September, Mrs. Phillips asked us to pick a hobby and to work on it during three half-hour periods a week. I had no hobbies. I woke up in the morning only when I had to, dashed through the morning routine, and ran out the door to school. In my haste, I usually forgot something and had to run back to get it before hurrying to avoid a red mark in the closed leatherette attendance chart placed carefully on the upper right corner of Mrs. Phillips' desk. I went through the day doing what I had to do, waiting for amusement at recess and lunch. I was not one to be the centre of attention, and my recent height had brought a number of second glances that I did not appreciate. I did my homework perfunctorily and was content to lie in front of the TV or read comics until it was time to crawl back into bed. It was an ordered life of sorts, if not an interesting one. My future opened blank before me and I waited for whatever might befall.

When Mrs. Phillips asked us to dedicate a few half-hours a week to a hobby, I was lost. I had no interests. True, I read action-hero comic books, but that only counts as a hobby when they're collected by an adult. Anyway, I didn't hoard old copies, but threw them away after I had read them a few times. The fact was, I had difficulty stirring up passion about any one thing. I took what came and made the best of it. So, when the moment came when I absolutely had to give a response to "What is *your* hobby, Ivan?" I blurted out without any forethought, "Stamps." The realization came right after, that now I would be expected to do something with this. "Stamps," I repeated, as if wondering where the word came from.

Now I was stuck. I knew nothing about stamps. The word had popped out under pressure, and when I was forced into a corner, I reached for the most ordinary thing I could think of, without the intervention of an ounce of imagination. Where does one get stamps? I had never sent a letter in my life. I vaguely remember being sat down once with paper to write a thank you letter to a forgotten aunt who had kindly sent me a gift. But I hadn't mailed the letter myself. I probably could not even find the local post office. Stamps. Now I had to do something with stamps three times a week. For half an hour. I had no hobbies, as I had no desire to disrupt the perfectly formless hours of my day. Stamps was my first foray into deception and its unforeseeable consequences. It was not a happy moment.

I looked up "stamp" in an old encyclopedia Walter and Macy kept on a small bookshelf. I read, "A postage stamp is a small piece of paper that is purchased and displayed on an item of mail as evidence of payment of postage." This dry description was not very informative and did even less to draw out my slumbering imagination. I saw a lot of wearisome articles on stamps and a few interesting pictures. The stamps in the pictures looked old, but I knew there had to be new stamps out there too. After all, my parents received letters every day with stamps on them. They did not often look happy to see the letters they received, and the envelopes remained torn on the table by the door with drab coloured paper jutting out from the jagged and hastily opened folded edges. Mostly they were bills, it seemed. Letters meant money. Spending money, not getting it. Letters were not talked about. Only bills were mentioned. Letters belonged to that unfathomable world of adults. Not my world at all, and not one I was in a hurry to discover.

With considerable difficulty — I had never had reason to use a phone book before — I discovered that there was a post office at the edge of my suburban realm: "Station Q" it was called, which I thought an odd name for a post office. It sounded like a galactic hub or interstellar docking station from a science fiction movie. The reality was rather more unassuming: a squat, flat-roofed, uninspiring square box of a building with concrete upheaving all around it and weeds interlacing the sidewalk. It looked untended, one might say unloved. The picture in the encyclopedia entry for "post office" showed an impressive stone edifice with a turret and peaked roofs designed, it was noted, by some eminent architect. But apparently such fantasies of public ornamentation existed only in a galaxy far, far away. Or in aging encyclopedias that would soon be eclipsed in their turn. Post offices were not to be found in my neighbourhood.

I tripped on the concrete as I walked up to the dull door encased in red aluminium, the defining colour of the Canadian postal service. The polished brass plates I had seen in the picture that were stamped with Royal Mail Canada and elaborate coats of arms above a ribbon proclaiming "a mari usque ad mare"—from sea to sea, as we had learned in school, proudly professing the great expanse of the country—were nowhere to be found. They were replaced by a solid red plate above the full width of the door with a stark blue ensign and very modern "Canada Post – Postes Canada" emblazoned in strict letters. A stylized, angular wing of what I took to be a paper airplane circled between the two national languages. "From anywhere to anyone" was the new motto. Well, I was "anyone," that was certain. And I lived "anywhere."

The storefront space was empty, except for a single employee. A row of neat letter boxes encased one wall, with a narrow table fixed to the floor in front. A sweep of cordon defined the queue for the absent clientele. I dutifully snaked my way along the grey floor and stood, waiting for the teller to acknowledge me. She twirled a white box on the tips of her fingers, eyeing the parcel as if a rogue element had entered her zone of command. Clad in the grey and blue livery of duty, she blew stray wisps of hair from her eyes to better examine her charge. Very suddenly she made a decision and flipped the box onto a raised counter behind her, jabbed at its surface with a large pen, and spun it into a cart hidden from view.

Having succeeded in dispatching the offending parcel, she turned her narrow eyes on me, ready to confront the next alien. She stood looking at me for a moment. I was tall, but my face was the face of a child. I think she could not quite decide what I was. I was sort of used to it. "I need some stamps," I said, looking her straight on. She hesitated a moment.

"What kind?"

What kind? That was a new question. I thought stamps were just stamps. I didn't realize stamps came in kinds. "Wha…What kinds do you have?" I stammered in return, buying time. It seemed like a reasonable question to pose in Station Q.

The young woman stared at me and chewed her gum. She shifted on her feet. "Like, what do you need it for? A letter?"

What else would a stamp be for? But I couldn't say that out loud. I felt at a distinct disadvantage. "Yes, for a letter," I said.

"For here or for the States or for somewhere else?" she asked, and then added, "How big is the letter?" Now I was in trouble, I could see. How big is the letter? I didn't know letters came in sizes. "Let's see your letter," she demanded.

"I, uh, don't have it with me," I said. Which seemed silly. I knew what she was thinking. Ivan the Giant was fading quickly into Ivan the child. Big boy. Big dumb boy. People expected a response commensurate with my size, and all I could do was give an answer commensurate with my eleven-year-old brain. It angered them.

I judged now that it was best to just explain myself. Dissimulation clearly was not working.

"I have to get some stamps for a school project," I said.

She looked at me blankly for a moment, as if this proposition were preposterous. Then she pointed to the plastic case under her finger. "What kind do you want?" she asked again, as if it might work this time with props lined up in front of her. "There's some here with the flag, some with the Queen. There's a series with World War II naval ships, and a series with Canadian artists' paintings."

I looked at the variety of stamps under my hand, protected in their plastic sheathing. I didn't know what to say. I was here for stamps, and there *were* stamps in front of me, but now I was expected to do something, make some sort of choice. I looked up at her, then down again into the case.

She saved me, finally. "Do you *collect* stamps?"

"Yes, that's it. I collect stamps," I said.

"This is the latest series," she said as she drew out a page of stamps with old war ships on it. "This is what most collectors are buying right now."

At last, a decision made for me. "Yes, I'll have those," I said.

"A page or a book of six?"

Another question. "Six," I said, paying from my unspent allowance and leaving quickly.

I was on my way. I had no idea what I was getting into.

* * *

My dad, Walter, helped me get on my way with the stamp hobby I was starting. He seemed somewhat indifferent to my plight of trying to satisfy a teacher, but then again, I was perhaps a little resentful about this foray into an unwelcome and hastily-chosen unknown, and my reluctance must have been felt by him. He was willing to help me find a stamp-collector's store, which I soon discovered was the place I needed to go rather than the local post office. There was one downtown, so on a bright fall Saturday morning we jumped in the car and wound our way out of the suburban clusters to the city. Our neighbourhood was as original as a stamp. Square houses, curved roads, planned ponds, and gravel walks through empty parks. Video games and student jobs had just begun to kill the neighbourhood camaraderie. We observed our neighbours occasionally over a white fence and smelled their grocery store steaks grilling on their Canadian Tire barbeques. Walter exchanged tips on tree pruning over the fence, and Macy smiled benignly at the neighbourly wife in a way that communicated a galactic distance across a space of ten metres. The neighbours across the fence left in the morning and their cars were parked in front of their house by evening. They had a dog that lived on a diet of special treats. A small child whimpered occasionally to protest. I had no idea what they did or where they went. But then if you asked me a direct question about what Walter did for a living, I would have been at a loss too. "He does something with pipes." It was a response sufficient for my purposes as I never strode into that part of his life. He existed as an adjunct to suburbia. He was necessary to my world. I liked the smell of his old sweater and appreciated the plodding way he kept my universe from collapsing into nothingness. Occasionally he informed me without preamble about some trivial but amazing detail, and I was astonished that he had such minutia tucked away under his broad and lengthening forehead. Fathers are surprising creatures.

We found the stamp collectors' store on a crowded downtown street that carried the sagging shoulders of its ancient and tiny buildings. Large dusty windows and peeling green paint singled out the stamp shop. A small step defined its individuality along the sidewalk, and an oval glassed door announced in curved, black Roman script, "Carruthers Collectors' Stamps." A bell on a faded red ribbon discreetly tinkled our presence in the hushed silence of the tiny public space provided to the specialized clientele. Sunlight streamed through the front window and rode particles of dust over heavy wooden and glass cabinets. There were books in the cabinets. It was not evident whether they were for sale or merely for consultation. Some seemed especially faded while others were new. There were few duplicates. We were glancing around the enclosed shrine to a man's ancient avocation and did not notice Mr. Carruthers, who appeared before us without sound or visible premonition. He seemed to gather form from the particles of dust in his shop. He peered at us from behind thick, round glasses that magnified the shape and size of his eyes. He blinked until we registered his presence. He was short and round without being fat and full. His face was pale and the skin seemed translucent in the borrowed sunshine that invaded his silent world. Even the street noise dared not enter this serious workshop that was the professional underpinning to a boy's hobby. Play and curiosity were translated here into serious study and patient application. A full head of wavy brown hair framed the round spectacles as he blinked until, surprised, we noticed him in front of us, behind an oak and glass presentation desk pressed under his stubby but articulate fingers. He was not there to serve, exactly, so much as to advise and mentor, and the initiative was expected on the part of those who entered rather than from him who ruled.

"Uh, hello," Walter began. "My son here is looking to begin a stamp collection."

Mr. Carruthers blinked his exaggerated eyelids and looked at me. He had to look up, as I was a full head taller than he. He did not seem perturbed by his inferior stature, nor did he let it convey any spectre of subservience. He glided in a plane above his varied clientele.

"Yes," he started. "And how far along are you in this endeavour?" he inquired, as if I were launching upon an expedition to the Antarctic and he was judging my relative state of experience. He did not look at Walter but addressed himself directly to me throughout the probing interview.

I looked up at Walter. "Oh, just starting, really," I said, coming clean from the start. My foray into this hobby at the local post office was still fresh in my mind. Better not to put on airs. Somehow the blinking eyes of Mr. Carruthers communicated to me that he would peer right through any childish subterfuge. "I started it as a project at school."

"I see," said Mr. Carruthers, a response which conveyed exactly nothing. "And what precisely are your intentions with this... project?"

I stayed silent, as the question made no sense to me. I was trying to fill up three half-hour periods a week. Stamps were a means to an end.

"That is to say," Mr. Carruthers continued, seeing that I was bereft of any sensible response, "is it purely for personal interest or might there be some more *professional* application?"

Dad was no help at this juncture. I knew I was deceptively tall and people made few allowances for my actual eleven-year-old emotional maturity, but Mr. Carruthers seemed completely oblivious to the equivocal human subject standing over him. Perhaps I took some small sense of satisfaction in the fact that condescension, at least, was an attitude entirely foreign to him.

"It's just personal," I ventured. And then, for some reason I cannot explain, other than that he had never ceased from looking only at me during this interview and never once glanced over at my father, I added, "However, if it turns out I enjoy it, then maybe I'll look into it more professionally."

In the periphery of my vision I could see my father's head twist to look me straight on. I ignored him. The transaction was between myself and Mr. Carruthers.

"Very well. For the moment your philatelic project will require three things. Firstly, some stamps. I would suggest you begin with a selection of British Commonwealth issue. Secondly, a stock book." He showed us a rather handsome hardbound book with black pages and opaque sleeves lined horizontally, behind which he slid an assortment of Canadian stamps produced for a Summer Olympics, showing me without explanation how to place the stamps in the stock book. He put a small plastic bag of stamps on top of the stock book once he had closed it. "These I'll give to you without charge as an encouragement to your, ah, project and as, ah, inducement to your, um, professional pretensions." He did not look at me as he deftly mentored my first step forward into the world of philatelic obsession. "And thirdly, you should have a catalogue describing the stamps you are collecting. This will allow you to research before you purchase again. One should not purchase without a definite intention in view, that is to say, without knowing beforehand what one wishes to accomplish by the transaction."

I cannot say I had associated stamp collecting with research and purposeful intent until that moment. But then again, I suppose it fitted in neatly with the object of a school project. I nodded. "Surely," I said, and I could see my father's head turn full on again. At that moment, I felt, finally, that there was something substantial behind my impulsive answer to a teacher's question.

"I will also give you a magnifying glass so that you can better examine your acquisitions," he said as he slid out a drawer from below the glass case, placing a large, round object before me. It was old, that much I could tell. Even while lying on the display case, it refracted the diffused light of the shop. A finely crafted silver rim encircled the leaded glass, to which was attached a smooth, pale handle that begged to be touched, caressed. I brought it up close to my eyes. "The handle is carved from bone," he said. "Elephant bone. It is quite rare these days. You may keep it as a present."

Mr. Carruthers raised his eyebrows almost imperceptibly, awaiting my reaction. All I could say was, "Thanks," which seemed inadequate, but my gaping mouth seemed to please him. He might as well have given me the treasured jewels of all the Rajahs of India, and in that instant, I would have traded all the comic books I had ever owned for that one artifact.

My father said nothing during this exchange and very little as Mr. Carruthers conjured up the materials from the dusty sunlight streaming in around us. My father paid the bill and we walked into the clear daylight. We walked silently back to the car. Although I could not articulate it at that moment, I knew without a doubt that a brick had dislodged from the childhood fortress that, until then, I had erected as a separation between my father and me. It was a feeling that flooded me with a sense of the future and the inkling of aspiration. I held the bag of promise in my left hand, and reached with my right to clasp my father's wrist for a moment and squeeze it tight.

CHAPTER TWO

All the way home, I resisted the temptation to look in the bag. Macy had an uninspiring lunch ready when Walter and I returned from Mr. Carruthers' store. The house seemed somehow brighter and newer after the glass and wooden shelves and the antiquated dust that had buoyed along the borrowed light streaming through the windows of the shop downtown. Here the air was clear, which made the voluminous rooms feel open, expectant. Rooms filled with the human presence of Macy and Walter who animated the spaces they called home and simultaneously glided through the inner chambers of my life. I carefully placed the bag at the foot of the stairs in anticipation of a more intimate moment when I might better review all that had transpired so unexpectedly during the meeting with Mr. Carruthers.

Lunch was a simple affair of finely shaved ham sandwiches and a bowl of thick vegetable soup to stave off the autumn damp. There was little conversation. Normally, I would have gone into great detail, hurriedly reciting the events that Walter and I had just lived through, but now, inexplicably, I felt unready to share the moment and could not give voice to the experience. Indeed, the experience, for the first time in my life, was not something that could be recounted by listing off who said what and what was done. The experience was incommunicable. Walter's silence. Mr. Carruthers' addressing only me, Ivan, and ignoring my father. The undertone of seriousness, the implication of much more than the interests of a simple recreational hobbyist, my own replies. None of that experience could be put into words. Walter must have concurred, for he, too, was subdued over the midday meal and seemed little able to enlighten his wife on the morning's events. I could sense Macy's eyes inquiring of Walter what had transpired between the two of us, and Walter's reply transmitted across the space that rested between all of us, "Not sure." The white bag sitting at the foot of the stairs with the stock book and sleeves bore proof to the successful conclusion of our expedition, but the content of the transaction was still lacking. I felt a little remorse that I was unable to share more of the experience with my mother, but I didn't know how to communicate the fact that, for the first time, really, I had been addressed without condescension or curiosity, but as... as... I just wasn't sure what. An apprentice? I suppose. Someone worthy of confidence. Someone who held in his hands the key to his own future. It was an unusual feeling, and no words I had ever learned stretched to cover its description. Macy reached over and stroked the fingers of my hand that lay quietly on the table, remnants of the gesture left to her as a mother who had once marvelled to unfurl the perfect, tiny hands and inspect the minutely formed nails of the being she had nurtured within her. She caressed my hair with her hand and looked at me as she always had, with a gaze that enfolded at once a sense of possession proper to a lifetime shared, and the respectful liberty that belongs to another being. I looked at her momentarily and smiled a word of reassurance.

I went up to my room. Dr. Seuss obligingly made room for Stanley Gibbons' *Commonwealth and British Empire Stamp Catalogue*. Although they remained neighbours on the shelf, the worn spine of *The Cat in the Hat* deferred to the venerable Gibbons. I opened the stock book with its black pages and passed a finger over the opaque sleeves, peering at the Olympic collection that Mr. Carruthers had bequeathed to me. I'm not sure if it was the meticulous and colourful rendition of heavily overpriced stadiums that enticed me the most, or the fact that a new acquaintance had entrusted them to me with confidence. The stamps conveyed a sense of worth. I placed the World War II ships commemorative edition with the small collection of Commonwealth stamps on my bed for later examination.

I pulled *Commonwealth and British Empire Stamp Catalogue* from its place beside Dr. Seuss. Stanley Gibbons produced a heavy book with high-quality images of the stamps that had travelled around the British Commonwealth in days when this represented something more than a cultural and historical link to the past, when the British "burden" to carry a civilizing influence around the world was felt keenly. Leese later filled me in on some of the details which manifested the motives of the men of power of another time, motives mixed with self-interest and self-effacement in that timeless concoction that whisks history along its contingent path. The images on the stamps were interesting and they reflected a burgeoning confidence, a message to circle the globe and announce that islands in a distant sea are real, and that plantations on a distant continent supply essential goods to the world. There were images of minute, colourful maps; of brooding colonial rulers; of exotic birds and circus animals.

Stanley Gibbons had laid out the stamps by geographical region in what it proclaimed in bold letters was the definitive and comprehensive guide, the one-stop shopping guide to the philatelic world. There were delicacies and oddities, the banal and the macabre, diadems and a bloodstained finger. I guess stamps were not just stamps. Now I was getting the picture. I would need more technical knowledge to tackle my school project. It seemed I needed to learn about watermarks and dyes, the history of print-making and the development of paper, plate flaws, retouches, monetary currency, and postal handling. I opened the small plastic bag with its "encouragement" of British Commonwealth stamps, and I pulled out a sleeve from the ring binder, a cardboard page with a clear plastic protector behind which Mr. Carruthers had slid the Olympic stamps. The cardboard kept the stamps flat and even. I took out a stamp from the plastic bag and examined it closely. It said Papua New Guinea. I had no idea where that was. I immediately associated it with the tiny creature in Tom's bedroom, a guinea pig. Perhaps this stamp held a clue to the origin of that red-eyed rodent that chewed vigorously at all the left-over paper rolls that Tom saved from a mundane destiny in the recycling bin. The stamp used a reddish-orange dye that I fancied came from the same earth that produced red rodents. The image was so intricate it was hard to take in all the detail with just the naked eye. "Halfpenny" was written below in thick letters and "Papua New Guinea" was inked confidently in bold, square script. I wondered if the confidence was borne out, as I still could not think where the place was, what it produced, or how it contributed to humankind. Maybe it had been prevented from contributing anything. Maybe, under the discipline of foreign masters, it was meant only to receive. I found myself wondering what had happened to the people in a country that, until that moment, I never knew existed. These were strange thoughts that strayed far from the mathematical coherence I preferred, but somehow these enticing speculations stoked a curiosity somewhere deep within that had lain dormant and untroubled since the dawn of my consciousness. Tomorrow was the next half-hour school period dedicated to our hobbies. At last I had something to bring.

Leese arrived at school each day early. I arrived each day as the bell rang. Tom arrived when it suited him, although he was rarely late, and when he was, he managed to charm the otherwise punctilious Mrs. Phillips out of an entry on the late-arrivals card. He did this naturally, without guile, which somehow made it acceptable to the rest of us even when we could never hope to court such favours. It provided us with a rare and amusing little spectacle and left us wondering where Mrs. Phillips stowed away her little exceptions, and in which coloured box-tray they were placed within the ordered system that structured her brain. "Very well, Thomas Andrew," she would say, using his full name to mark the solemnity of the grace he had received, "but just this once. We mustn't make a habit of it."

"No, Mrs. Phillips," was all he had to reply. In fact, more would have spoiled the entire effect for us all.

Today I arrived early. Leese was already there. Tom, no doubt, was on his way.

"I started my hobby," I said to Leese.

"Stamps, right?" she said and I nodded. Leese was putting together a printed collection of historical documents. She said she liked the look of the old parchment and the red wax stamps that sealed the handwritten documents. Strange hobby, I thought. I wondered what went on in that mind of hers, what obsession with the motives of human beings ran rampant within her head. Still, she *looked* pretty much like all the other girls.

"I'm having trouble reading some of the old documents I found," she said.

"Mmm." Not easy to know what to say to that.

"They used old-fashioned quills and real ink. And penmanship was very different back then."

Penmanship? Quills? Didn't I use real ink? "Mmmm."

"Tom said he's going to work on something to do with science," Leese said, as she glanced down the street to seek a sign of his arrival. "No idea yet, though. Maybe he came up with something overnight."

I rocked back and forth on my heels against the chain link fence that defined the perimeter of the school's world. One breached the perimeter only at defined times of morning and afternoon. Other students were gathering in the yard, some standing quietly in the chill, others already embracing the day. Movements and shouts grew in frequency and intensity as the thin morning light gradually released its energy into the huddled air of autumn dawn. Still no Tom.

The bell rang and Leese and I hung back as long as we dared, expecting a trotting Tom to cross the threshold just in time. But he was not there.

Mrs. Phillips was arranging the day for us and working out the routine preambles which started each morning like an overture to the organized rhythms that patterned the hours. She kept looking at Tom's empty chair and tapping distractedly at the corner of her desk. Usually, within the first two minutes of the day, she opened the fake leather folder that held our attendance cards. She was obviously buying time. The overture was lasting longer than usual. She was outlining in greater detail than was customary the classes we would be following that day, reminding us of a need for diligence at all hours and holding out the carrot of a last half hour of dissipation over our chosen hobbies, like a reward for sitting straight with feet flat on the floor. Slowly, reluctantly, her hand moved toward the attendance folder that remained always at the top corner of her desk. She finished speaking and, uncharacteristically, let out a very slight sigh and then said nothing. In that suspended instant the door flung wide open and Tom teetered in with a cardboard box balanced precariously in front of him, cantilevered against the weight of his body. He was out of breath.

The box was closed on top but bursting the seam of sturdy grey duct tape that held it in check.

"Sorry, Mrs. Phillips," Tom wheezed. "I had to… carry this box… all the way… from my house."

"Well, Thomas Andrew," Mrs. Phillips began, clearly relieved that her strategy had not been foiled, "we were just getting ourselves organized. Take your seat and we will get on with things." Tom was trying to slide the box on a table at the back of the classroom. "You haven't missed anything, so I suppose we can let it go this time. But we mustn't make a habit of it."

Tom replied on cue and in all earnestness, "No, Mrs. Phillips." It somehow pleased us all.

Then, like a trainer having narrowly escaped calamity with an unpredictable circus animal, Mrs. Phillips stepped confidently forward to take control of our day. "Our first period is math."

Normally, the abstract arrangement of numbers would have consoled me, reassured me that all could be regimented by finding a common pattern. But that morning I was too distracted. Papua New Guinea kept coming to mind, with its bold letters and reddish earth-ink. Where was it? Who lived there? What did they do all day? Did they have their version of Mrs. Phillips to structure the hours of the morning? Twenty-four hours ago, these thoughts would never have come into my head. Was I turning into a Leese? I looked up at the long timeline of human history above the blackboard. Where did Papua New Guinea fit into that version of historical events? Had its people not contributed to the advance of human culture and knowledge? Did they not rate a picture on the world scene?

The day mooned on and I continued in a half-daze, the world taking on new forms and my thoughts erring through a forest of unfamiliar trees. Tom and Leese looked at me from time to time in a strange way. Or maybe they just looked at me as they always had but everything now looked strange just to me. Finally, the last half hour arrived, the hour consecrated to our hobbies. I pulled out my stamps and books, pouring over the foreign world condensed to figurative representations on tiny rectangles of coloured paper. The older stamps had a dull finish, the ink lacking the lustre and shine of the recently printed. Was the world duller too back then, or had it just been given a modern gloss in our day?

Leese brought out some printed reproductions of ancient monographs written in barely legible script, ornately squashed into wobbly horizontal lines. Flourishes of florid penmanship at irregular points marked the documents with supercilious originality. Images of red wax seals pompously affixed to the bottom by a scratchy signature lent an official air to the works.

"Look, this one seems to be a will," Leese said, holding up the photocopy for inspection.

"Mmmm."

Tom's bursting box had rested on the counter throughout the day. Now, he elaborately began peeling the bands of tape holding his box together. "At first I was going to work on my bug collection," he said. "My mom started it when I was five and I used to add to it when we went away on holidays." I tried to imagine Alice's fashionable fingers clasping a black beetle frantically swimming in the open air, a captive to childhood fascinations. It made for an incongruous scene in my head. "But then when you said you were doing stamps and Leese said she was investigating historical documents, I thought of something else. What's the common denominator between you and Leese?" Tom asked. Leese stood beside us. She stared blankly at Tom. I didn't have any input either. "Paper!" Tom exclaimed. Leese and I continued to stare at him. "Paper. You know, stamps and ancient manuscripts, they both use paper."

"I suppose," I said. Paper was something you threw away. I didn't see paper as a subject for hobby making.

"Remember when we were studying the ancient Egyptians and they used papyrus for paper?" Tom asked.

"And the Chinese used rice," added Leese. She was starting to get the idea. "This will was written on parchment," she said, inspecting her photocopied document with renewed interest.

"Look at your stamps," Tom said. "Look at the tiny lines on the paper. They had special dyes, too, to get the colours to stay on even if the letter fell in the ocean before it was delivered. I was looking into it a little. Did you know that they had to develop special techniques to produce some of the stamps at that time?"

I looked at my stamp book again. It is true I had been looking only at the pictures that were produced from around the world. I had not thought of the paper on which they were printed. And the colours, too, I had noticed, but I had not associated them with scientific techniques of colour dyeing and mechanical reproduction. Trust the science guy to notice that.

"There are all kinds of special papers for different things. Artists use acid-free paper made with a lot of cloth in order to have the dyes stick properly and not distort the colours. Museums frame their paintings with special cardboard. My dad was looking at some original blueprints from my grandmother's old house and the paper was really smooth and the ink was this weird shade of blue that looked like it had seeped into the big sheets."

I remained doubtful. But then, Leese and Tom looked at the world differently from me. I suppose that was a good thing. New perspectives and all that — what educators kept telling us. Tom brought out some small screens he had been experimenting with. He needed a mesh on which to "set" the mashed pulp while it was still wet.

"I haven't made anything yet that could be used. I've just been experimenting with different types of pulp. I've used up just about all the paper we've thrown out at home. It's like the ultimate recycling project. Dad's happy."

I could see Rick crouched like a bent straw inspecting Tom's work, and Alice demurely in the background rummaging in the closets for old paper and rags.

"I haven't really started into the dyes. I have to work on the right consistency for the paper mush first. The dyes have to be made from natural things, and if the paper isn't consistent, the dye will take unevenly. It's actually kinda int'resting," Tom said as he caressed one of his screens and ran his fingers along the mesh, then poked his finger in the middle to test the tension. "Hmmm," he said distractedly.

Leese took a few more samples of documents from her backpack. They were in a clear plastic folder separated in individual pockets like a silent accordion. She had a selection of wills, she stated matter-of-factly, the human being's attempt to prolong life after life has ebbed, wreaking havoc or charity according to strictures of justice or caprice, wherever an errant heart beat its last retreat. Why do we always insist on having the last word? "Look, this one left everything to a niece in Guatemala…" The writing was not easily read. It was formal with curved capitals and forward leaning letters that somehow ran together while fighting to remain distinct. Great letters three lines high began significant phrases, the whole thing officiously impressed with a great disc of red wax sealed by the letter "J" in an elaborate setting of wavy lines and curly ends. "J" obviously had thought a lot about what would go on after he had ceased gracing the Earth with his worthy presence. He felt the weight of his responsibility to hold the world together from the grave and dispense his beneficent suzerainty from the throne of a granite tombstone. Well, it was true his parchment had made it into history for the general edification of succeeding generations, so maybe he had been on to something after all.

I looked at my stamps that had raced around the world in the last hundred years, spreading news of the new world to the old, raising hope again in an age of cynicism, and boasting of the progress of human effort. It didn't change the fact that I still didn't know where Papua New Guinea was. But that was my fault, I guess. I took an atlas off the back shelf in the classroom and shifted through its pages littered with orange and blue and red. Papua New Guinea was colonized when ships were the vessels of discovery, and I sailed my finger over the great reaches of blue, condensed and distorted to fit on a large page. The pilgrims of adventure would have tucked away a cargo of sheets of paper, parchment, wax, and stamps, all necessary to the exploration of new lands and the communication of novelty to the wearied world they had left behind. Stamp collecting was opening up a horizon of endless vistas, imperceptible until now in the fog of my listless brain. An unaccustomed stirring of adventure pulled somewhere from within.

CHAPTER THREE

———◆━❖━◆———

I returned home right after school and hunted through the kitchen cupboards for some cookies or chips. It was an after-school routine that I had assumed as a little reward for getting through another day, a deserved rest from the pretended heroism of my less-than-extraordinary life. I was, in fact, quite exhausted from unfamiliar thoughts and feelings that had moved within me during the entire school day. I sat listlessly at the kitchen table and stared at a plate of cookies, hunched over with my elbows on the table. Macy and Walter would be home soon from their daily adventures in papers and pipes. I could hear the short screech of the mailbox by the front door. Letters had arrived. Not rice paper or parchment laden with cold wax, not ancient testimonies in faded script wandering and racing forward off the page, or tales from far away and exotic lands, but bills mass-produced on reams of industrial chlorine-bleached paper, perfectly spaced, set in Times New Roman typeface — and stampless. In the commercial world, stamps were replaced by a simple pre-printed acknowledgment of "evidence of payment of postage." Envelopes existed merely to be torn open and abandoned by the front door until Walter and Macy finally had to pay out the neatly prescribed "amount due" by the "due date." The only fantasy that came through the letterbox was the brightly-coloured advertisement for changing one's cable provider or the enticement for a trial subscription to a glossy magazine, and even these were hardly personal. They found their way to the kitchen garbage without any detailed appreciation for their commercial art.

I finished my snack, picked up my bag, and went to my room. I threw the backpack on the bed and threw myself after it, sprawling and rolling over onto my back, staring up at the ceiling with a drugged lassitude. The stippled ceiling stared blankly back without enlightenment. I turned and opened the pack and pulled out my stamp collector's tools. The "British Commonwealth issue" had shuffled around on its neat stock book cardboard. I had been careless when I put the stamps in the protective covering. Mr. Carruthers would have written off any "professional pretentions" right then and there if he had known. I lifted up the stock book and shook the stamps onto my bed. They fell in disarray over the eyes and face of Captain America. I was into comic-book action heroes. The rust-coloured islands of Papua New Guinea stared up from the cheek of the hero printed on my bed sheets. Nightly, I had wrapped myself up in imagined tales of the struggle for justice and the protection of the innocent, not to mention the salvation of the world. Captain America stared up at me with Papua New Guinea licked to his cheek. Here was adventure of a different kind, maybe even real heroes no one ever talked about, sailing over blue seas to stormy lands of unknown threats under the hushed rumours of cannibals. The scent of death is somehow necessary to any true sense of adventure. Comic books know this as much as real-life, the only difference being that comics have a pre-determined end, and one always wakes the next morning flinging Captain America back to start the day with victory already in the air.

I looked past the islands and the bold lettering designed to make a statement and catch the inquisitive eye. I touched the paper that faithfully had held the coloured dye for many decades. It was rough, not smooth. The commemorative stamps I had purchased at the drugstore postal outlet were glossy and self-adhesive like a label on the cellophane wrapper, meant to be glanced at, torn open, and thrown away. Purposeless bits of coloured film intended for a moment's curiosity. In contrast, Papua New Guinea's "Halfpenny" had travelled who knows how long and how far, and still the ink was clear and the letters striking. It was designed for enlightenment, not curiosity. One felt somehow richer for having received it, and shied from casting it aside. It had passed over my threshold now and was in my grasp. It still served its purpose.

While the paper was not glossy or hardened with a superficial gloss, its texture gave it its slightly rough feel. It did not slide between the fingers but held its place securely by its tangibility. I looked closely and noticed horizontal lines — ridges, really — on the crafted square of paper. The ridges were discernable enough that they gave a patterned shading to the orange-ochre dye. The eye could detect the shadows from the ridges and so the colour seemed not uniform, but an alternating line of dark and light, so delicate as to be unnoticed at a casual glance. There was art in the paper as there was consideration in the choice of dye. A letter from Papua New Guinea in the 1930s would not likely have flown; it would have floated across the globe, at least in part. The risk of damp and heat were calculated in the production of something so small and insignificant. Someone had chosen the image; someone had taken the time to design it and set it for printing to a minute scale. So much thought in such an ordinary thing. I felt ashamed at the thoughtless hours I so easily surrendered each day. There could be obsession in the ordinary and masterwork in the mundane. The proof was that this tiny piece of art still existed and I could now hold it between my thumb and forefinger, wonder who had crafted it, and wonder, too, what I could learn about this strange land that was announced to me unannounced on the corner of a torn envelope that had never been any larger than a scrap of tissue.

As it turned out, Tom was on to something with his curious hobby of paper-making, a hobby, no doubt, as invented on the spur of the moment as mine, but with a little more imagination. The research I began during my initiation into stamp collection revealed very quickly that paper was a key factor in establishing the authenticity of a stamp-collector's claim to having uncovered a genuine article. A lot of money could be at stake, many thousands and even millions of dollars. But the paper on which the stamp was printed could not be faked. Images, even ink, could be reproduced according to authentic techniques, but paper, the ancient and humble medium of human communications and art, could not. There was carbon dating, of course. But more importantly there were processes of paper-making that corresponded to eras and historical periods. Elaborate forgeries relied first of all upon finding paper from the era and even the locality of the authentic stamp. Paper-making needed three key ingredients: water, pulp, and mesh. Water carries impurities typical of a region, and pulp was produced most simply by soaking plants and natural cloths like linen in local waters until a soggy mess was produced. The pulp was poured over a wire mesh and then dried, leaving the imprint of the type of mesh used. Rustic papers used coarse mesh, but with time paper-makers developed fine wire mesh with regular patterns. Individual paper-makers could design their own mesh which would give a very delicate textured finish to their product and identify their craftsmanship. Quality paper for writing a last will and testament was not cheap in centuries gone by. It needed to be smooth for writing, capable of being folded without breaking or tearing, absorbent for ink but not to the point of destroying the delicate furls of seventeenth-century penmanship, and resistant to humid summers and dry winters. There was science and technique in paper-making. It was a craft that developed its own experts with their secrets, and patents meant profits. In Great Britain, a government contract for paper-making "by appointment to His Majesty's Royal Philatelic Offices" was as lucrative as discovering a galleon of Spanish gold.

I became obsessed with researching my hobby. In fact, it is fair to say that the simple collection of bits of square imprinted paper was not the enjoyment. Possession may bring a certain satisfaction, but the chase was all the fun. I was astounded to learn, very quickly, that it was not necessarily the quality of the materials, design, or execution that created value, but rather the *im*perfection. Here I was spending all my time trying to perfect things and now I discovered that faults in a fragment were the real bearers of promise. Human error did not always result in tragedy. Human error gave spice to the chase of things. Uniformity brought certainty and predictability, but what every child knows instinctively is that what we truly seek is the deliciously unpredictable, the hope of uncertainty even as we go about our predictable lives. Every now and then the threat of uncertainty is what gives a complaisance to the certainty of the day. We take rest and comfort in the ordinary, but we delight in the unpredictable. Some try to substitute the unusual for the unpredictable, but this is a mistake. Novelty is never defined by the weird and aberrant which are merely gross exaggeration, but by the subtle alteration of what appears, at first glance, unoriginal and unexceptional. Hope never wanders far from the humdrum.

An inverted letter, a dot out of place, a dropped "s" or a lifted "t" were the Spanish gold of stamp collectors. It was the printer's imperfection that created excitement, before the error was noted at the central desk and quality control was reasserted for the next run of stamps. Later, I would understand better this general principle of art and craftsmanship. The ancient Greeks, we were told, knew how to create pillars which were not perfectly vertical in order to respect the natural distortion of the human eye, so that the curved lines would all merely *appear* to be straight. The structural integrity was not lessened by the imperfection; nevertheless, the total effect could not be summarized by its physical integrity only, but in technical specifications moulded to human aperture. The play of the human was designed into the mathematically correct, like the placid grimaces on gothic statues that expressed serenity in a convoluted world, their "s" shaped figures molded in unnatural but graceful curves. The forgotten artist was not content to imitate life in all its perfection, but crafted the human body to the laws of a geometry that defied skeletal structures. The jutting hip of a saint supported the corpulent body of a child grasping at a perilous fruit in a maternal curve that communicated both safety and liberty. The grace came not from the natural form but from the artist's pliant hand. And yet the human form was evident and rendered somehow more beautiful through its imperfect stance.

I lay sprawled across Captain America, eyeing with renewed vigour the details of my British Commonwealth issue. I looked beyond the outlines of maps and the intricate colouring of rare birds to the stuff on which they were printed. The colours and details seized the eye, but the imperceptible ridges left by fine wire mesh demanded touch. The colours were raised to life from the fibre of the page. It was remarkable, really, what effort was spent on such a tiny commercial form.

Walter and Macy entered my reveries when the house shuddered as they closed the front door behind them. Macy came up the stairs and sat on the foot of Captain America. "How was your day, hon?" My mom put her hand on the top of my head and brushed stray wisps of hair from my forehead. It was not possible for me to articulate, but it was a gesture which I liked, a touch which reassured. I did not turn my head to stop her.

"Good," I said. "We had a half-hour period to work on our hobbies at the end of the day." I rolled onto my back and looked into Macy's face. Her hair was pulled back from her face and her forehead glistened. "Tom's into paper-making and brought all kinds of stuff with him. It looks complicated."

"And what is Leese interested in?" she asked.

"Ancient manuscripts. She had copies of some old wills and it was almost impossible to read the way they used to write. Lots of swirls. Actually, it was kind of interesting." This was an admission more to myself than to my mother. She smiled. She, at least, was still able to look beyond my outsized body to recognize the boy within. She could see beyond the grotesque.

"No basketball today?" she asked. Practice was tomorrow.

I did some homework with the stamps littered around me on my bed. The inclination to distraction was strangely lacking.

I walked downstairs for supper and passed the small table in the hall. More letters had been ripped open and left carelessly for later consideration. I picked them up. No real stamps, only inked facsimiles. I walked into the kitchen and listlessly snooped around the counter where Macy was putting the finishing touches on the meal in an efficient if relatively thoughtless manner. She was not an adventurous cook, which was fine since I was not an adventurous eater.

I wandered to the table near the counter. On my plate there was a letter placed neatly with its long horizontal edge parallel to the oblong table. I looked at Mom, who smiled and continued with efficacious intent applied to the salad in front of her. The envelope was not white, but a tan colour. Leese, no doubt, would have described its hue as that of parchment. I picked it up. It was an envelope meant to be touched, not torn open, with horizontal ridges closely packed and vertical ridges about three centimetres apart, perfectly spaced. On the upper right-hand corner there was a stamp. Not a glossy, self-adhesive one like a bandage one wraps around a cut finger, but a matte surface with a picture of the Queen. As I had learned, the Queen's face had recently been redone to show her age.

And her dignity, I suppose. It was not appropriate for the Queen to smile. Nor to frown. Constitutional monarchy is a serious thing embodied in a monarch who is born to it, not chosen, least of all by mere mortals.

The letter was clearly addressed to me. It was not typed, Leese would be happy to see, but inscribed with a perfect penmanship. No curlicues or meandering lines. It was contemporary but timeless too. A lot of practice had gone into writing my name.

I turned the letter over, a ridiculous gesture, but somehow natural. An embossed return address discreetly printed on the closure flap indicated without pretension but with great assurance that it originated from the hand of Mr. Arthur H. Carruthers of Carruthers Collectors' Stamps. Walter entered the kitchen and looked at me with the vague outline of a smile. I couldn't remember having received a letter addressed uniquely to me during the whole of my life. Anything to do with me had always been sent through Walter and Macy. Arthur H. Carruthers, it seemed, did not put much stock in protocol.

It seemed inappropriate to tear the letter open. One who had spent such time preparing a letter deserved a little more consideration. I fetched a knife from the drawer and slid it under the flap, neatly drawing open the closed envelope. The tear left miniscule shreds of what appeared to be very fine linen threads. I would have to show Tom tomorrow.

The letter inside, which I slowly unfolded, was written on only one side in the same neat, timeless yet current script that had drawn my name. "Dear Mr. Morrow," it began. I was eleven, so this was a shock. "I wish to thank you for your patronage of Carruthers Collectors' Stamps and to encourage you in your new endeavour. Many persons have found philately to be a satisfying, enjoyable, and even intriguing avocation, and I hope that it will provide you also with a source of pleasure. I encourage you to pursue your nascent interest with thorough research of all aspects of stamp-making in order to draw out the full satisfaction it can provide. I am available for consultation at any time. Please do not feel bound by the hours posted on the window of the store. I can be reached at the telephone number listed below if some urgent request should arise, as happens from time to time." It was signed simply, "Sincerely, Arthur H. Carruthers, Ph.D., Philatelist."

I handed the letter to my father without a word. "Well, that's kind of him," was his only remark. He explained the contents to Macy and handed the letter back to me. "Put it somewhere where you can find it again," was his only comment. Until now, Walter had been my only secure treasure of vital information. It was he who kept the records of birth, death, and religious affiliation locked away in his brain or filed away in the box tucked into his closet. My job was to *ask*. His job was to *keep*. I could see that this, too, was about to change. Mr. Carruthers had initiated yet another Copernican revolution in the life of my domestic affairs.

As we were eating our way through Macy's version of stewed beef, Walter interrupted my rather long-winded account of the day. "I just remembered something I had completely forgotten. It's strange, but your great-grandfather collected stamps. I remember the books on a shelf in his study." My great-grandfather had been a history professor at a local college. He had written a well-received book on the Anglo-German naval race leading up to the First World War. It was filled with dreadnoughts and statistics and diplomatic communiqués with just a hint of espionage. Until now I had not inherited any of his passion for history. My father read an occasional heavy tome about people long dead who had pulled at the strings of fate or providence, with sometimes happy results, sometimes tragic. I was satisfied with numbers and make-believe. Captain America provided a routine dose of drama and thrill.

"In fact, it's been so long now I haven't given it any thought for years." He paused. Macy and I weren't quite sure how to respond, but he continued soon enough. "It's strange. He gave away his stamp books to a young collector just before he died. I was only eight or nine at the time, and none of his grandchildren was interested in his hobby. But apparently, he kept one small bag of stamps. He told your grandfather, my dad, that it was not to be thrown out, nor under any circumstances given away, but kept until someone in the family could appreciate it. He made my father promise, and my father made me promise. We've kept it here. It's somewhere in the basement, I'm sure." He paused again. "Curious. I never gave it much thought."

After supper, Dad, Mom, and I descended into the jumble of our basement. Disused furniture and the discarded remnants of early life lay tumbled together waiting for a garage sale. No one had gotten around to sorting through the stuff.

We rummaged through boxes and big tubs without success. Walter exclaimed from time to time, "I know I put it here," and Macy replied, "Well, it's a good thing we are hopeless procrastinators."

"Pathological hoarders, you mean," corrected Walter.

The place was disorganized before we had entered, but now broken stools, limbless tables, and horrific pastel fashions were strewn in complete disarray. Tom's bedroom looked like a well-catalogued museum by comparison.

Walter let out an "Aahhhhhh" as he clutched and then shook a purple felt pouch at us. "That's it!" he exclaimed. The gold letters stitched into the fabric said "Crown Royal" — Canada's whisky.

He threw the pouch at me and I clutched at it in my hands. It was soft and filled with shards of paper. "I don't know why he was so particular about it, but it must have meant a lot to him. We were all to wait until someone came along who also took stamp-collecting seriously. So, I guess that's you." I shook the bag which was held tight by a golden drawstring.

Taking the bag to my room later that evening, I poured out the contents and shuffled them about with my forefinger. I did the math. There could be nothing in there dated within the last forty years, more or less. At some time before that, there had been a king, not a queen, then there had been the Second World War followed by the Cold War, satellites spinning round the Earth, and the moon as the last frontier. I wondered idly what state Papua New Guinea had been in forty years ago. There were stamps with bearded effigies of several different Georges, a stamp to declare those victorious in combat, and stamps numerous enough to provide the identifying labels for a whole botanical garden of exotic flora. Kings, wars, and gardening, the pastimes of an earnest society.

Most of the stamps had been carefully unglued from their envelopes, but a small number remained on torn scraps of envelopes, indicating dates and post offices of origin. Someone, presumably my great-grandfather, had spent a lot of time dissolving the glue so as not to damage the integrity of the stamp. It was monotonous work, although I had not yet tried it. It might require the patience of more than an eleven-year-old. I held some of the stamps up to the light and they turned opaque in my fingers.

One could detect the fine filigree of the paper underlying the image and the uneven dye that created the illusion of shadows and perspective in miniature. The images of kings were largely monochrome, often a grey-green. The flowers burst with lines of colour, preserved from fading in the dark felt bag that had served also to prevent humidity from destroying the fabric of the paper.

Of the stamps still affixed to their envelopes, most were dated between 1937 and 1949. One had originated in Pennsylvania and I wondered about my great-grandfather's connection with that state. While most of the envelopes were of a grey unbleached colour using thin paper designed to decrease weight and so the cost of shipping, one stood out as brighter and smoother than the others. Any writing yet discernable on the envelopes was handwritten with a fountain pen, but this one alone had fragments of a typed address. It was more of a commercial correspondence than personal, and, curiously, it was postmarked 1957 from Belgium although the stamp was English. The pattern was broken. A letter out of place. It could not have been done by chance, and, I fancied, it was done to communicate something. This was something that a serious collector would notice. This was something that would incite his curiosity and demand an answer. I held the envelope up to the light. The paper remained transparent but the stamp did not. Like a photo negative, the stamp was dark when held up to the light. I examined it more closely. The stamp seemed unusually large, although not so disproportionately large that it would stand out. It could be easily passed over. When held up to the light again, and looking through it from what would have been the inside of the envelope, it was clear that the edges of the stamp showed slightly more transparent than its centre. It almost seemed like a square within a square. I clasped the stamp between my thumb and forefinger. It was slightly thicker than it should have been. Very carefully I rubbed a fingernail up to the edge of the stamp. Nothing. It held fast. I brought the stamp up close to my nose and examined all four edges. It had a vaguely musty smell, like an old book ignored for decades on a dusty library shelf. I could see no edge ready to peel away or slightly unglued over time or by design. I bent the envelope so that the stamp stretched over the seam. Then I slowly bent it in the opposite direction, so the stamp was forced into a convex "U" and it became clear that only the edges were glued to the envelope since the centre of the stamp bubbled up. Not wanting to tear the stamp in two, I slowly strained it back and forth in concave and then convex motion. Suddenly the bottom right corner came loose. I laid the envelope flat and held my breath as I slid my fingernail up against the loosened edge. In a single moment the entire edge pried open and I could clearly see that there was another stamp lying hidden underneath. I felt the blood pump around my ears and heard my breath shorten. The stamp underneath was not glued to the envelope and it slid out without damage. I stared in astonishment. Captain America lay coolly impassive by my side.

CHAPTER FOUR

———◆━◆━◆━◆———

The stamp was old but in perfect condition. It had the face of a young woman, presumably a queen, with a thick necklace round her neck, and it was entirely printed in black. In each corner was printed "12" just outside an oval black border that framed the oblong face of the elegant woman and in which was printed "Canada Postage Twelve Pence." When had Canada gone from pence to penny, I wondered? I brought out my treasured magnifying glass to look closer. Caressing the smooth bone handle between my fingers, I felt like a sleuth from another century gleaning tiny clues from shreds of evidence. The printed image of the stamp was accomplished by a profusion of very small, individual dots of ink spaced closely or at a distance in order to produce the effect of shading and light. It was much like a painting we had studied at school where instead of brush strokes the painter painted with thousands of points, each point a different colour like a miniature mosaic. Up close, it was impossible to see the shape of the figures, and they revealed themselves only when one stood at a distance. From a distance, the eyes were tricked into seeing chiaroscuro circles or ovals artificially given three-dimensional still life as apples or precious gems or children bathing at an idyllic seaside.

The lady had a slender neck and oval face and she stared into a space somewhere to the left of me, regally ignoring my intrusion into her tiny portrait. There was no defect to behold, no crease, no stain, no tear, no indication that the stamp had actually been used. No tell-tale wavy lines printed over top to indicate that it had been processed on a regular envelope. It looked new in its perfectly preserved oldness.

The envelope it was hidden on was ordinary, a fragment of a whole. Whatever typewritten print that remained was torn now and it was impossible to tell to whom it had been addressed or from where. The Belgian postmark alone revealed its origin but the stamp betrayed a mystery since it could not have been used to post the letter. If the letter had been posted from Belgium it would have had a Belgian stamp on it, but the large stamp pasted on the envelope and hiding my Canadian stamp was English. A stamp was evidence of payment, of pre-payment, to be precise. Until 1840 in England, it was the person who received a letter who had to pay upon delivery. The great innovation was to permit pre-payment of correspondence, and this gave rise to the printing of stamps, small tokens pasted on the newly invented envelope as "evidence of payment." We take it for granted, but stamps and envelopes were revolutionary in their day and led to a boon in postal service, the development of an entire industry and, with it, a new form of commercial art. The simple stamp reduced the cost of letters by leading to their profusion, bringing them within reach of all classes. The demand for paper increased, as did the need for paper of a lighter weight so that more letters could be carried in the same volume of shipment, which increased efficiencies and reduced costs further. It was a happy result that kept friends and family in touch across counties and beyond oceans. The invention of ocean-going steamships reduced the time needed to send a letter and spurred global enterprise, facilitated far-flung diplomacy, and promoted the centralization of bureaucracies dedicated to the fluid governance of growing colonies half-way across the globe. Stamps were invented to smooth the flow of prosperity, and although they may have become an item created of necessity, they quickly became icons of pride and ornate manifestations of power, prestige, progress, and profit. The artist dabbling in the popular production of miniature engravings of the grand masters found a new outlet for his talent and a prospective source of income. The commission received to paint the portrait of the Queen proved doubly lucrative when that well-used image was reproduced as authoritative guarantee of pre-payment on a common stamp, spreading the notoriety of the artist and prudently foreseeing a contractual stream of income in the form of royalties.

All of this background information, of course, I did not see when I peered intently at the curious stamp for the first time, but Mr. Carruthers' insistence upon research would take me beyond a boy's hobby and the caprice of a dilettante. My great-grandfather had the inkling that he possessed something unique and he had taken pains to see that it was not lost, even if he had been unable himself to capitalize on it. He had preserved his little treasure, confident that a moment would arrive when some distant offspring would understand what was to be done with it. It seemed unlikely that it should come to me, but I held it now between two fingers as I wondered where it would lead me.

I pulled Stanley Gibbons' *Commonwealth and British Empire Stamp Catalogue* from its shelf beside Dr. Seuss and randomly flipped through its pages. I had not yet familiarized myself sufficiently to even know where to look. I felt helpless in the face of the mystery woman.

I lay back, cradled in the two-dimensional embrace of Captain America, and wondered what to do. I stared at the ceiling which looked blankly back at me, a white, horizontal plane that seemed to border onto an infinity that promised no answers. Questions upon questions upon questions. Hobbies are meant to be distractions, escape routes to flee the habitual. I had chosen the most ordinary hobby and now the ordinary was opening up a space within me that had lain undisturbed for eleven years. I didn't quite like it, but I could neither ignore nor close it up again.

I remembered Mr. Carruthers' note and I searched for it on my desk under the textbooks, comics, and stamp books. It lay under Dr. Seuss, which I must have removed from the shelf when reaching for Stanley Gibbons. "I can be reached at the telephone number listed below if some urgent request should arise, as happens from time to time." Mr. Carruthers had written that I need not feel bound by the hours posted on his door. It was now evening, long after the shop would be closed. Evening openings and extended hours were not part of the Carruthers business model. It was almost 10:00 p.m. The phone number was on the bottom of the letterhead. I hesitated, then went into the hall downstairs and found the phone. It was an older, heavy, cordless model. I took the phone to my room and dialed the number. It rang exactly three times before a click was heard and the distinctive voice called down simply, "Arthur Carruthers. May I help you?"

"Hello, Mr. Carruthers. This is Ivan Morrow. Thank you for your letter." At least he would have to acknowledge that I had been well-raised. Macy was very particular about telephone etiquette, and the small toy phone she had bought me as an infant had been used many times so that basic manners with strangers would become second nature. Mr. Carruthers was appreciative of my gratitude.

"Actually, I have a little question and I was wondering if I could come by the shop to discuss it. It's about a stamp I received from my great-grandfather."

"Your great-grandfather?"

"Yes, he left it to my grandfather and then my father. In fact, a whole collection of stamps. I was looking through them this evening and would like some help identifying one of them." I automatically eased into a different phraseology with Mr. Carruthers, effortlessly departing from the vocabulary and tone I assumed with parents and friends. I remarked the change in me, but was powerless to prevent it. Mr. Carruthers simply demanded a new idiom.

"Certainly. Can you come by the shop after school tomorrow?"

"Yes, I was hoping to do that."

And so it was arranged. I hung up after a polite exchange of promises to see him tomorrow. It had not even entered my plan to ask Walter to call Mr. Carruthers, or even to show him the stamp. Somehow stamp matters had become a domain restricted to myself and Mr. Carruthers. Parental involvement was peripheral. I checked out the bus routes and counted out the change I would need for the trip out of the suburbs the next afternoon. Forethought and planning were new to me, but it was accomplished with a new naturalness I did not question.

The next day at school followed its predictable routine. Mrs. Phillips tapped out the rhythm with polished nails and we heeded orders. Tom had stained his hands when working with some dyes for his paper the night before. His fingernails were a phosphorous, pale violet, which he ignored and everyone else remarked upon. Leese was hunting down a history of signet rings that were used to press an image onto the red sealing wax used in previous centuries. She was thorough in her research, which was unsurprising but rather wearisome to listen to. It was not one of the days that ended with a half-hour hobby time. I was disappointed and, at the same time, rather surprised at my disappointment. I had told no one about my discovery. I needed first to reveal it to Mr. Carruthers. I needed some real facts to go on and was reluctant to speak of it while my own research remained unfinished. The lady in the stamp disdainfully stared beyond me. I needed solid information before discussing her.

I had rarely taken the bus and never on my own. My oversized body now proved a distinct advantage. Travelling alone on public transportation while still a child is inadvisable, but now no one mistook me for a mere child. I entered the world of adolescents and adults as I stepped up into the bus. No one looked at me like I was out of place. I sat beside a girl with very black hair. I was anonymous and inconspicuous. It was my first realization that what was exceptional within my little world — my height — was unexceptional in the wider universe. I relaxed and enjoyed the transition out the window from wide empty boulevards to cramped, centre-city streets. Cars moving, cars parked, people walking, people standing.

The door appeared the same as the first time I had entered it, a step up off the street with the little shop's opaque air within. This time Mr. Carruthers was at his windowed show-box, as if anticipating my arrival.

"Good afternoon, ahhh, Ivan," he said from behind a cloudy curtain of dusty air.

"Hello, Mr. Carruthers." Hello was not a word I usually used.

"So you have inherited some stamps." I did not think of myself as an heir, but made no correction; Leese was the one concerned with parchment and last testaments. "And you would like some advice on what you have discovered."

I had brought with me the little felt bag stored among generations of worthless household items. I removed it from my knapsack and put it on the glass-topped showcase between us. We both looked at it. "This was my great-grandfather's collection." I reached into the bag and pulled out the envelope. I had restored the queen to her hidden realm where I had discovered her because I thought, somehow, that it would be important for Mr. Carruthers to see exactly how she had come to me. "This envelope was in the bag, but something seemed not quite right." I pointed to the Belgian postmark.

"Ah. Very curious. Clearly postmarked from Belgium, to be sure," he said. "But then, why the English stamp?"

"Well, yes, that's what I wondered when I saw it." I then bent the envelope slightly to reveal the hidden stamp beneath. I pinched the stamp between thumb and fingernail and drew her out from hiding. Mr. Carruthers drew a sharp breath, and in the serenity of his own realm, calm was shattered. He opened a drawer from beneath the show-case and pulled out a pair of tweezers, lifting the stamp with trembling fingers onto a black velvet pad.

"Extraordinary." His finger hovered over the image, wanting to touch but not daring. He raised the black velvet close to his eyes and examined the tiny figure for several minutes. Placing it back down, he continued to gaze upon it. "Beautiful," he said. "I have never seen such an exquisitely preserved original of this stamp. See how black the ink still is, no fading." He looked into my face and then back at the face of his queen. "Lovely." I stood still, not wanting to break his moment of rapture.

He drew a long breath and asked, "Do you know what it is?"

"No," I said, "I am not yet expert enough at the book to be able to locate it." Then after a moment I continued, more as an affirmation than as a question, "It's valuable, isn't it?"

"Very," Mr. Carruthers replied. "In fact, it is considered, at this moment, the most valuable Canadian stamp on the market. There are very few, and fewer still in such pristine condition. See, there are no perforations along the edge. The stamp was printed on a long sheet of paper, called classic laid paper, which was the common type of paper at the time. It has a texture. You can see the horizontal lines just faintly, and one vertical line here," he said, using the tweezers to point out a barely discernable raised line slicing downward through the right cheek of the queen. "This one's never been used. Instead of separating the stamps by a perforated edge, this stamp has a straight edge, and someone at the post office had to cut each stamp from the larger sheet. This one seems to have been from the left corner of the full sheet, because the left-hand border and the bottom border are much larger than the top and right-hand side. So the person simply snipped this stamp from the others printed to the right and above it." I realized this was an obvious observation, but one which had escaped my untrained mind. "I believe that one sold some years ago for about $300,000.00. It was used, although in very good condition. Today it is estimated that it might fetch at least double that. And yours is in mint condition. Yes, it is very valuable. If it *is* authentic." He paused. "They do not come on the market often, as there are so few of them. It is hard to say just how much it would fetch today. The novelty of a new find would, of course, augment the interest."

He turned the stamp over. "The gum — the glue — on the back is intact, as you can see. Very unusual. It has never been used." He paused. "The history of this particular stamp is relatively clear. It was printed in 1851, ten years after the two original Canadian colonies of Upper and Lower Canada were united. Do you know your Canadian history?" He peered at me.

"Not very well," I admitted. I was sure Leese would have had something to say where I did not.

"Well," he continued, "Canada gained its independence from England slowly over time. By 1851 the United Provinces were granted the right to issue their own stamps, so this is one of the first that was printed under Canada's own name. That is why it very proudly says, 'Canada Postage.' It was a significant statement for the colonials at that time, like a rite of passage. They wanted to assert their growing independence from the British Crown, but they could only do so carefully, so they undertook to print their own stamps. They still took pains to put the queen's face on it, since they couldn't discount their allegiance to the British Empire just yet." Mr. Carruthers smiled to himself as he paused. "It is thought that 51,000 of these stamps were printed at a printing press in New York. That's the face of Queen Victoria on the stamp, and I wonder what the Americans would have thought about producing this image of the successor to their former oppressor." He smiled again, this time at the irony. He continued speaking, but it seemed he was speaking to himself. "But I suppose payment is payment, and, besides, they had won their independence seventy-five years before. Thus time — and perhaps money — heals all discord." He continued after another moment, "The value of the stamp was twelve pence — the Canadians did not yet have the right to mint their own currency. Twelve pence was a very large sum in those days, at least twice the standard rate to send a letter to the United States. There were few who needed stamps for such a large amount, and few who could afford them, so it seems that most of the stamps were deliberately destroyed six years later. Only 1,450 are known to have been in use. Yours is one of those."

I looked at the haughty face of the queen. She had a name now, Victoria. Queen of England and so Queen of Canada. I thought, too, of my great-grandfather who had hidden this stamp away. "Is that why my great-grandfather had hidden it away? Was it always so valuable?"

"Not really, not until quite recently. It has long been a collectors' stamp, which may explain why your great-grandfather took such pains to hide it away. Ingeniously, I might add. The English stamp on a Belgian post-marked envelope is a stroke of genius, an obvious clue to those acquainted with philately that something was amiss here that required further investigation." He stopped and looked at the stamp again, then continued, "You recognized something was wrong, didn't you?"

"Well, yes," I said, "but I didn't know what, exactly."

"That's the starting point for all worthy investigation," Mr. Carruthers nodded. "It can lead to great discoveries when handled properly. You have made a very significant find, here, Ivan. Very significant indeed."

I'm not sure if it was the tone of his voice or the fact that he called me by my name that lent the note of importance to his words and invited a new confidence in me.

"Does your father know what you have found?"

"I haven't told anyone. I wasn't sure what it was." And it was true. Whereas before I would have shared such a find with Tom and Leese without a second thought, everything had changed since I had first walked into this shop. My relationships were altered with my parents and with my friends. Only a few weeks ago, I would have burst with the news, spilled it out to my friends, and thrown the whole incomprehensible chain of discovery into the logical competence of my father to be sorted out. I would have waited for an answer. Waited for someone to tell me what it was all about. Waited for someone to tell me what I was to do, which was the next step to take. But now… Now *I* had to find the answer. I felt a certain responsibility to my great-grandfather who had waited for this day. I felt an obligation to the trust confided in me by Mr. Carruthers. But there was something more. With thoughtless disregard for consequences, I had made a decision, ironically, to escape from the responsibility of decision-making. A decision to collect stamps. Not an ounce of thought or imagination had gone into that decision. At the time, I was not even conscious, really, of having made it. I just sort of fell into it. But it was made and now I would have to see it through. What was my next step?

Mr. Carruthers seemed to have anticipated this peculiar new attitude. "You may keep the stamp with you, of course," he said, "in which case you must keep it somewhere safe. There are many people who would be interested in what you have found. And there are some who would take measures to obtain what you have."

Parents were for safekeeping if anything important came along. Where would they put it?

"On the other hand," he continued, after hesitating a moment to inspect the royal gaze in more detail, "I have some little experience with matters of this kind. I have, over the years, amassed a significant collection which is of considerable worth." He looked up at me and then down at the rarity I had produced so guilelessly. "It would be possible for me to… uhhh… keep it safely for you." He stopped and looked up at me through magnified eyes behind thick lenses. He peered into me, it seemed. I was uncertain what he was searching for. I suddenly felt extremely uncomfortable. Uneasy.

My life had been made easy until this moment by the trust I put thoughtlessly into those around me. I had shifted the responsibility to others without forethought. As he scrutinized the workings of my mind in that moment, I realized I had a real decision to make. And real consequences would follow from that decision.

His gaze shifted away as suddenly as it had stolen into my private sphere only a moment before. I shifted on my feet and stared down at the queen, but she had no wisdom to impart. It was up to me.

"I think I'll hang on to it for now," I said, and scooped the likeness back into the velvet bag.

"Ahhh. Well," was all he could say.

"I should head back home now," I said. I stopped for a moment and looked into his eyes, but I could read nothing there. His hand had flinched as I pinched the stamp from the top of his display case, but he controlled his movements. He rapped the glass surface.

I turned and fled the store.

CHAPTER FIVE

he bell on the faded ribbon clanged noisily through the glass window as I abruptly shut the door and stepped down onto the sidewalk. I looked to the right and the left, a little confused. I could feel the stare of Mr. Carruthers' magnified eyes search my indecision. So, I stepped to the right with a confidence that was more apparent than real. Unfortunately, it was the opposite way to the bus stop so I had to wind my way around the block, by which time I had recovered some of my composure. In the knapsack on my back was a promissory note for at least $600,000.00. It was a sum that meant very little to me. It was a sum that was unreal, and I had no need of that much money, even if I knew what it really meant. If it had been two one-hundred dollar bills I might have had a better grasp and, perhaps, more anxiety. I was thinking, rather, of my great-grandfather. Somehow it seemed as if he were placing me in a position of trust and responsibility. This unknown, unfaced, and faded ancestor. The queen's face seemed somehow more familiar, and yet I felt as if I owed something of great value to my great-grandfather, and not just the price I might obtain for the stamp, but the custody and safety of the treasure he had entrusted to me.

The bus ride passed more quickly than I expected and I scarcely noticed the landmarks out the window, almost missing my final stop. I was anxious to arrive home before Walter and Macy so as not to have to explain my delay. They could see through any lie. But chance was with me and I arrived to a quiet home and closed the door behind me. I do not think I had ever appreciated the staid and monotonous security my parents had afforded me as much as I did at that instant. The suburbs brought a welcome anonymity.

I ran up to my room, threw myself across Captain America, and closed my eyes, lying there thoughtless for a while. Finally, I got up and went into the bathroom, opened then closed the cabinet, and shifted things in the drawer below the sink until I found what I needed. Tweezers.

Back in my room, I emptied my backpack and pulled out the queen gingerly with the tweezers, careful not to touch her disdainful face. I stared at her for a very long time. I must keep her in a safe place. But where? Where in an eleven-year-old's room is a safe place? I reached for Stanley Gibbons' *Commonwealth and British Empire Stamp Catalogue* which I had taken with me to Mr. Carruthers. I found the page at last where the young queen was described in rather terse, concise language, but I now knew all that was written there. I was about to release her from the pinch of the metal tweezers when I had a second thought. Wouldn't that be an obvious place to keep the stamp?

"Keep her safe," I said aloud to Captain America. I looked around my room. Nothing obvious revealed itself to me as an appropriate treasure chest. Not where she could get wet if I spilled a drink. Not where she might tumble out if moved when tidying up, or sucked into darkness down a vacuum tube. My eyes roamed around. Somewhere dark so she would not fade. Somewhere dry so she would not rot.

My gaze landed on Dr. Seuss. I hadn't opened those books in an age. Not since I was six or seven, perhaps. Not an obvious place. I had several of his books, worn from repeated use years ago. I pulled one off the shelf, my favourite — *One Fish, Two Fish, Red Fish, Blue Fish* — and opened it up, releasing my queen next to the winking eye of a blue fish.

Some are red and some are blue.
Some are old and some are new.
Some are sad.
And some are glad.
And some are very, very bad.
Why are they
sad and glad and bad?
I do not know.
Go ask your dad.

But I would not ask my dad. Not yet. My adventures of the afternoon passed unknown and unmentioned over supper. A day like any other.

At school the next day, too, I kept silent. I was unsure what to do. I needed some sort of plan before I revealed the extraordinary turn of events to Tom and Leese. I remained distracted during Mrs. Phillips' forays into math and history.

She had to call me from my thoughts which had drifted far from a lesson on feudalism in the Middle Ages. Kings and princely knights, vast green vales and castles with wide moats, rough-clad vassals pledging oaths of fealty. Little did she guess that I had a queen of my own. A regal, disdainful, haughty, linen-faced queen sequestered deep within the great towering keep of an innocent child's book of verse.

Tom and Leese glanced at me from time to time with a curious and inquiring twist of mouth and brow. But I did not yet know how to let out the strange turn of events of the last day. We ate the conforming lunches of the suburbs, the white commercial bread gumming the inside of our teeth, wiped clean with the tarty juice of new autumn apples. Leese was explaining some document she had just found, while Tom took the opportunity to wax eloquent on the chemical nature of parchment which enhanced its qualities of preservation. My mind was numb and the details and facts washed over my brain without imprinting any form or matter. I brushed aside an invitation to spend some time after school to visit Tom's paper distillery, a messy arrangement of sluicing boxes and knotted linen remnants. I needed a little time to myself, although I was not at all certain that I could make profitable use of it. My next step was a blank and I really had no idea what I should do next.

Today was not a hobby day and lessons ended with the shriek of a bell, but Mrs. Phillips advised us as we were putting books in desks and paper in backpacks that tomorrow we would each report on the progress of our hobbies. It would be time for "show and tell."

I returned home quietly and sought the solitude of my room. I lay on my back and stared at the ceiling for a long time. Homework was not on my agenda and, besides, I would not have been able to concentrate on anything. My predicament consumed all my energy and thoughts, but without producing a single productive conclusion. I did not rescue Her Majesty from the captive clutch of blue and red fish with long eyelashes. But I could not quite figure out what to do with her.

Walter and Macy came home and remained quiet downstairs, checking in on me without the invasive questions on the progress of my learning that day. Just as well. I would not have been able to report any satisfactory development. Supper was ready early and I shifted downstairs as my mother gave a final flourish to a comforting fall meal. I was surprisingly hungry. Words fell about the table in a hesitant and disjointed manner. School, work, news. The usual stuff, but terser. Sentences stopping and starting, thoughts begun without bringing to conclusion their full expression. Finally, my father looked over at me, right into my eyes. I stared back. This was usually not good, but I did not sense any danger. He looked down and said, "Mr. Carruthers called me today." It wasn't so much a statement as an invitation. I remained dumb, struck by a sense of... I wasn't sure what. Betrayal? But, of course, it was only reasonable for Mr. Carruthers to inform an eleven-year-old's parents about a treasure unearthed, even if he had only dealt with the child when initiating it into the world that had led to the discovery. "He says that you may have discovered something... of substantial interest."

"Of substantial interest" was not a Walter phrase. I could hear Mr. Carruthers speaking. I didn't know what to say. Silence.

"He said it was something of great value, if authenticated."

"Great-granddad left it in the bag you gave me," I said, finally. "It was hidden on an envelope. A 'Penny Black.'" I looked at Walter and Macy. "Queen Victoria. Mr. Carruthers said it could be worth $600,000.00 or more." I hesitated, "If authenticated."

"We'll have to look into it," Macy offered. "Where have you put it?"

"In my room. Hidden."

We went up to my room and my parents glanced around. They, too, wondered where one hides a world-class stamp in an eleven-year-old's room. I let them look around for a moment, then reached for Dr. Seuss. "Clever," was all my dad said, and he smiled. I took the tweezers and revealed my queen. 'I do not know. Go ask your dad.'

"What do I do with it?" I asked.

"I have no idea," Walter replied. "But we don't keep it here. I have a safety deposit box at the bank. We can put it there tomorrow."

I explained about the show and tell at the end of tomorrow's school day. Walter said he would be there. He said he would accompany me. Someone had to carry the stamp. And then we could go straight to the bank and safely store our dubious treasure until we knew how to proceed to have the mysterious gift of a distant grandfather evaluated. A wave of relief washed over me. Finally, a plan.

Walter stayed home the next day as I trundled off to the schoolground. He would bring the stamp at the end of the school day. I met Leese on the school grounds. Tom, of course, was not there yet.

"I have a whole series of documents that show the progress of record-keeping from the time of the Magna Carta," she advised. These are just copies," she said as she thumbed through her colour reproductions, "but my dad helped me find a *real* one. It isn't anything valuable, of course, just something we found for sale. We can't quite read the writing, it's so cramped. But it's supposed to be a will from 1849. It has a real wax seal on it. Or, at least part of the seal; part of it fell off. The paper is pretty delicate and you have to wear white cotton gloves to handle it. The ink is quite faded and blotchy in parts. It's French, from after the French Revolution."

"That's really interesting, Leese," I said. I really meant it, actually, but I didn't feel it. She sensed the hollowness in my reply.

"Well, it should be a good thing to show this afternoon." It sounded like she was trying to convince herself. Perhaps, after all, it was possible for someone like Leese to have something akin to self-doubt.

The conversation drifted and dried up, and I felt I wasn't holding up my end of the effort. "Sorry, Leese," I offered. "I don't feel much like talking today."

She fumbled with her knapsack which stood on the ground at our feet. She looked up and around. Just a bunch of kids playing a bunch of kid games.

"There's Tom," she said as the school bell disrupted the cold morning air. "Just on time." We waited for him to trot up and went in together.

Mrs. Phillips stood at the middle of her desk surveying us all as she tapped once with her index finger on the black attendance folder. She looked at Tom and seemed pleased. Or at least satisfied. The day was off to an ordered start. From within the middle drawer on the left side of her desk she produced the book we were reading. It was not the done thing for a boy to say, but I enjoyed *The Secret Garden.* True, I was a little annoyed by things like scarlet hibiscus blossoms, and the description of vegetation that meant nothing to me in my semi-arid, northern plains existence and which had to be looked up each time in a dictionary. Which I didn't do. It interrupted the flow of immersion in the old world of the author with the ancient name, Frances Hodgson Burnett. Still, from the very first pages, I have to admit I was captivated by the "child no one ever saw."

"What person did Ms. Burnett write it in?" First. "What is the mood of this section?" Indicative. "How does she develop the character in the opening sentences?" By describing her face as disagreeable and saying she was always ill. "Is Mary Lennox a sympathetic character? No? Why not?" Because she is selfish and tyrannical. "What language does the writer use that makes you dislike her? What words?" She was a "selfish little pig," a phrase which I particularly liked, since I knew quite a few people I thought would fit that description. Of course, I couldn't say that out loud, but it was nice to read it and think it in the freedom of my brain. "Where is she going with this, if Mary is the protagonist?" Maybe Mary has to change her disagreeable temper through the unfolding of the story. Don't we all have to change at some point in our lives? Looking back, I have to thank Mrs. Phillips for my appreciation of literature and the powers of critical analysis, and perhaps a little, too, for coming to understand the idiosyncrasies of human nature.

"Do Mary's actions accurately reveal her thoughts at this point?"

That is always the real question, isn't it?

The day wore on and I wondered when Walter would appear. I felt somewhat disconnected from events after the excitement of the previous day. I should have been eager to reveal my discovery, excited to show the others what I had uncovered. A little vain, perhaps, that I could trump them all. But as the activity swirled around me, it failed to catch me in. I spoke little and munched on peanut butter sandwiches that clogged my throat. Mrs. Phillips did not seem to notice that my mind was somewhere else most of the time, which, I suppose, was the advantage of being only one amongst thirty-two in a classroom. She needed to end the day with the ordinary accomplishments of texts analyzed, sums added, and experiments written up. My actions, at least, did not betray the inmost confusion of my thoughts, although perhaps my silence did. Then again, I had once been described in my report card as "lethargic," so, in my case, excitability would have been a sort of betrayal.

Walter slipped into the class as Mrs. Phillips was telling us to put things away and bring out the evidence of progress in our hobbies. To my surprise, Mr. Carruthers eased in behind him. Mr. Carruthers was out of his world in this sparkly realm of Mrs. Phillips. The sunlight made him blink through his thick glasses. He glanced around this foreign territory, a necessary excursion from his dusty domain. Did *his* actions reveal his thoughts at this point? What would Frances Hodgson Burnett do with him? Or with Walter, for that matter?

My father held both my stamp album and the catalogue of Mr. Stanley Gibbons. Mr. Carruthers carried a locked briefcase that was of worn brown leather but obviously solid. He held it with both hands. Both he and my dad remained unmoving with their backs up against the classroom wall, as if Mrs. Phillips had placed them there for some sort of detention. The delict of showing up where they did not belong, perhaps. Everyone stared at them.

But Mrs. Phillips was not to be put off from her purpose by any intrusion.

One by one the students explained the hobbies and what each of them had accomplished since the start of the school year. There were hockey cards and pressed flowers, model cars and kits of military ships, dolls and tiny lead soldiers. Each of my classmates had something interesting to say, which surprised me. Cards were no longer just cards imprinted with popular or famous faces, but transmitters of a vast array of detailed statistics that traced the history of sport. Dried flowers preserved the painstaking hours spent transplanting seeds from exotic lands and nurturing them in an unhopeful climate. And stamps…? Stamps were proof that exotic lands existed far away, that mankind hoped for universal recognition, and that great-grandfathers had secrets which transcended generations.

My "exhibit" produced the most excitement. It wasn't really the stamp that caused the swirl of students around my desk. After all, it was only a tiny portrait in blank ink on authentic paper such as one can no longer buy except at great expense, but it generated excitement because it was an original discovery. And of course, because it had happened to me, who had been, up to this point, simply a classmate, and not a very original one in any possible meaning of the word. Tom used the magnifying glass brought for the purpose by Mr. Carruthers to inspect in great detail the quality of the fine paper mesh that captured the artist's efforts to reproduce a queen using tiny black dots. He had a rather long conversation with Mr. Carruthers, who, it turned out, was quite an expert on what Tom was messily trying to produce in his sluice box. Tom was astounded at Mr. Carruthers' knowledge and, no doubt, at his manner of expression, which allowed no adaptation to Tom's suburban vocabulary. Even Leese was suitably enlightened on the qualities of parchment when she finally had occasion to probe the professional collector's mind on the issue close to her heart.

All the students gathered around and then Mrs. Phillips organized them into an orderly queue with a ten-second allowance to view the stamp individually. But when that was done, they all simply crowded around Mr. Carruthers and my father, who acted as custodians of the remarkable legacy. Mrs. Phillips herself looked quite impressed with my exhibit, which was no mean feat to accomplish. She was not someone overly impressed with the efforts, possessions, or imaginations of eleven-year-olds. She allowed herself double the time of individual allotment to peer at the valuable stamp. She had no words for Mr. Carruthers, but looked him up and down (when he was not looking) as if sizing up his capacity to deliver what he pretended to be. She must have resolved in his favour because she stood aloof while he fielded questions from my classmates.

When this was accomplished, Mr. Carruthers placed the Penny Black into the stamp book. Leese placed herself right in front of him and almost tugged at his shirtsleeve to pull him over to Tom's sluice and her own parchment, which he declared to be made from sheepskin, finely rendered into a vaguely translucent film that had weathered and coloured to a soft beige over the years. As for the seal, he was unable to place it because the image it bore was broken, but he said it resembled those used in the duchy of Savoy, which was only annexed to France in 1860. By the end of the day, Leese felt her exhibit had gained some merit, and perhaps herself as well. She sniffed a lot.

Mr. Carruthers came back to the table, placed the stamp book in his worn but sturdy case, and locked it securely before taking leave of Mrs. Phillips, who was, perhaps, not accustomed to his formalities, certainly not within the walls of her own classroom. She recovered herself sufficiently to thank him for coming and for explaining so thoroughly the history and value of my exhibit, and to issue a monition to me to guard it safely and to inform the class of the results of the evaluation. Then she nodded to my father, and the three of us left the room.

It was rare for me to see the inside of a bank. Walter was my bank. I followed my dad to the vault where the safety deposit boxes were cloistered. On a table placed for viewing contents, Mr. Carruthers unlocked his briefcase and opened the stamp book. He flipped through the pages and grunted, then flipped through several more with something of a look of concern. Then he turned up to look at my father and blinked his eyes.

"It's gone!"

CHAPTER SIX

———◆━◆◆◆━◆———

Mr. Carruthers checked through his briefcase once more in great detail. Nothing. I felt a little sick, not so much because of the lost stamp, but because of the strange feeling that I had let an ancestor down. Someone whom I had never met expected something of me and, in way, had a claim on me and on my attention. I felt responsible, although I knew I had done nothing positive to cause the loss. It was not what I had done, but what I had *not* done that had made the difference. A moment of inattention. Until now my life had been woven from moments of inattention, but always I had been saved from the consequences of neglect by the adults that hovered around me, teachers and parents, mostly, who plucked me from the abyss of childish and indulgent negligence.

Walter looked bewildered. Mr. Carruthers looked shaken.

We retraced our steps to the school but the day was out, the students were gone. A few played outside in the crisp autumn afternoon, voices shrill and echoing. The classroom was open and we entered without much hope. Such a small piece of paper. It could have fallen anywhere. We walked around the room and lifted papers, books, and all the remnants of a child's effort to learn about himself and the world around him. The young queen had absconded before she could reveal herself as true or untrue. Or had been kidnapped. But there would be no ransom note. We investigated in silence the circumstances of her last appearance.

Mrs. Phillips flew into the room with a great gust of determination and almost toppled over when she saw we were there.

"You gave me a fright!"

None of us found a word to respond.

"I was just coming from a teachers' meeting to straighten up."

Mr. Carruthers cleared his throat and peered at Mrs. Phillips for a moment. "I think it might be a good idea if you rather did not straighten up today, Mrs. Phillips."

She stared at him as if such a sentiment were incomprehensible.

"It's my classroom, Mr. Carruthers."

"Yes, but a very valuable item has gone missing and it would not do to disturb things until it is found."

"An item gone missing?" It was clear that in her world things simply did not go missing.

"Perhaps misplaced?" Mr. Carruthers ventured in a rare display of accommodation. Misplaced might just be conceivable.

"Did you or did you not put the stamp book with the stamp in your briefcase, Mr. Carruthers?" I had heard that tone many times. Usually it did not end well. I wondered vaguely how Mr. Carruthers would get himself out of this difficulty.

"That is what I thought I had done."

Silence.

"Evidently, that is not what happened."

"Well, then, it must have fallen out at the bank. Or on the way to the bank."

"Yes, but it appears it did not."

"So, then, you think it must still be in my classroom?"

"That would appear to be the logical conclusion."

"Well, I'm not sure if it's the *logical* conclusion of an act of neglect, but we can have a look just the same."

"We have just been through things here, and we have, as yet, not produced the missing stamp. This is serious. If authentic, a great discovery has been lost."

"So you explained to the children. But this is my classroom and I will see what is out of place." She proceeded to move about the room with a curious attention to the smallest detail. She looked in and under things we would not have stopped to consider. A ruler was perched on the back shelf and she shuffled a few books. A child's desk was twisted out of place and she opened the top to peer inside at the contents. She let out a disheartened sigh. A pair of shoes was stranded in an aisle and she picked them up to return them to the rack at the back of the room. It was the first time I looked at the room from the eyes of my teacher. They opened upon a world different from the one I was used to noticing.

"I really don't know," she said. "I really don't know. Nothing here seems to indicate a lost stamp."

"Yes, that is my thought as well," said Mr. Carruthers. Walter remained subdued and he seemed relieved to have Mr. Carruthers present to face Mrs. Phillips. "This is a terrible blow not just to Ivan but to the Royal Canadian Philatelic Society. Such a discovery is rare indeed."

"Yes, I suppose it must be. Shall I leave the room as it is?"

"If you could do so, that would be very helpful. And if you might tell the evening staff not to clean the room until I have been able to go through it again, I would be very appreciative."

Mrs. Phillips hesitated and seemed to fight against the reasonableness of the request. Her eyes struggled to admit that one morning without perfect order might be allowed. Under the circumstances.

It was at that moment that the school principal, Mr. Marjonson, peered in. In a few, but well-articulated, phrases, Mr. Carruthers explained the situation to the principal. A "Dear me" settled the issue and the room was locked and a sign taped to the window on the classroom door. "Yes, yes, of course," the principal responded to Mr. Carruthers' request to return the following day for a further inspection. Mr. Carruthers assured Mrs. Phillips that he would come early, before the school day began, and he and Mr. Marjonson arranged the details. The classroom would remain locked until then. Mrs. Phillips seemed less pleased. Indeed, she seemed a little put out. A queen must assert her dominion, it is true, but there are limits even to regal power.

She was even less pleased the next morning when it was apparent that Mr. Carruthers had arrived with not just a few friends to thoroughly search the room, but with two police constables who, it appeared, had been through something like this before. Mrs. Phillips so far lost her presence of mind that she did not even remember to take attendance that morning, and her organizational powers abandoned her when faced with students thrilled both by the hearing of my loss and by the rather novel experience of trying to sit still while the representatives of Her Majesty's Royal Constabulary finished picking through the ruins of a grade six classroom. Mrs. Phillips' desk was a wasteland of collected shreds of paper and debris that had been placed there by the constables as mysterious clues to the disappearance of the young Queen Victoria. My father was there too, and I had come with him early to accompany the police and Mr. Carruthers. Still, the stamp remained missing.

Mrs. Phillips did not improve with the day. We were left to ourselves as she managed only the barest outline of a day's curriculum, and we bathed in the freedom of a forced holiday. Mr. Marjonson dropped in a few times, but to no real effect. He was used to such unplanned occurrences, although perhaps never before in the realm of Mrs. Phillips.

Tom and Leese were beside themselves with glee and tried to hide behind clumsy phrases of concern.

"Do you think they'll find it?" Leese asked. "I'm sure the police will find it." But the disappointed tone of her voice seemed to want that they would *not* find it.

Tom was less trusting of constabulary efficacy, but he made reassuring noises that it should turn up eventually. He thought it was a good thing it happened in our classroom where things were generally in order. After all, if it had been in Mr. Maugher's science room, the stamp might have ended up as bedding for the hamsters and that would be that.

For my part, I wished that Dr. Seuss could have kept the Penny Black for a little longer. It seemed, in hindsight, safer with him than with anyone else, except, perhaps, my great-grandfather.

From near to far
from here to there,
funny things are everywhere.

But I kept my thoughts to myself.

One thing I *had* noticed as the police were rummaging about the room was that the black leatherette attendance folder was not on Mrs. Phillips' desk, which might explain why she hadn't bothered to take attendance. I assumed that the police had confiscated it. Tom, at least, would be happy.

Order was restored by the next morning and the preliminaries began as usual with taking attendance. The attendance folder was in its correct place and the shreds of paper from the top of Mrs. Phillips' desk were nowhere in sight. Mrs. Phillips, so far from the dishevelled appearance she put in yesterday, was more alert than ever and relished the reestablishment of her rule with decided satisfaction. Even Tom suffered. He had to fetch his attendance card from the office before being admitted into the classroom. Truancy was a misdemeanour not to be overlooked today. For anyone.

No quarter was given to the distracted, indolent, or merely unlucky. It was rough going and we all felt we had put in a full day by the time the last bell rang. The last half hour normally dedicated to our hobbies was cancelled in favour of a revision of math. Which was fine with me. I preferred not to think about what had happened to my stamp. Sums were orderly and always concluded with precise, sober certainty. Leese could have her world of adults and their history. "Glum" was not a word which frequently leapt to mind, but that is how I felt. Glum. It had a Dr. Seuss feel about it that suited my mood.

Blue fish
Glum fish
Red fish
Lost fish.

I shunned the suppressed excitement of my friends and settled into a decidedly peevish mood. Which was not like me.

Walter and Macy could not placate me. An eleven-year-old pout is about the most intractable of human dispositions. The child can neither be distracted by dangling a coloured ball before the eyes nor moved by appeal to nascent rationality. It is a world of in-between. Toys suddenly reveal themselves as just toys and not representations of a fantastical world. Yet the responsibility of adult concerns is still not fully perceived. This in-between world raises its own inner logic, indefinable and yet compelling. It can still glimpse the world as the child before the man, and disrobe the clever machinations that men imagine they impose. It is, in truth, a world that remains close to reality, for that is all it has ever known. Until now.

A vanishing stamp is simply not real. Not in the circumstances of yesterday, at any rate. This much was clear to me. It simply could not happen. That was all I knew. And that knowledge made me peevish.

So how to go from There to Here, as Dr. Seuss might ask?

I went over the events of the show and tell in my little classroom. I peered out the corners of my memory's eyes but could see nothing unusual. My strength was in finding the order in things and in discerning the predictability, not, like Tom, seeking out the one thing that does not fit. My gaze sought out regularity, patterns.

Adults acted responsibly; that was their pattern of behaviour leading to predictable outcomes. So, at least, my experience told me. Under what circumstances does a responsible person not act responsibly? I had not been a responsible person all my life. Perhaps I had an advantage here. What would an irresponsible person do?

My great-grandfather had hidden the Penny Black with intriguing complexity for who-knows-why. Was that a responsible action? Impossible to calculate at this distance without knowing his circumstances. That he knew he had something worth hiding was clear. Why he chose to hide it was another thing. Was it a curious game? Was he worried about losing it, planning to bring it out again at a later time, perhaps in a time of need, but then death intervened to thwart his plan?

A responsible person would carefully hold on to the stamp in a safe place for safekeeping. Dr. Seuss, for all his ingenuity, was not really a safekeeper, except perhaps to an eleven-year-old with peculiar notions of security.

Where would a responsible person responsibly guard a valuable piece of paper? How could I possibly answer that? Especially if the valuable thing was stolen and could be easily identified. Whoever had violently taken possession of my Queen Victoria would surely know that if it turned up in their possession, it would be definitive proof that they had taken it illegally. It was a mathematical certainty and an irrefutable conclusion. So, then, the answer must be: steal the valuable but not keep it in one's own possession. Yet they would still need to get it when they needed it. How to possess something but not to possess it at the same time?

It was a fitful sleep that night with vague dreams of queens and capture and release. None of which helped. Or came to pass.

CHAPTER SEVEN

F or the first time in my life, I arose with a sense of determination. I had no plan, which wasn't unusual in itself. But I had a sense of resolution, which was completely new. My fingers tingled with the novelty. I jumped out of bed, throwing Captain America disdainfully aside. I couldn't ever remember jumping out of bed before. Dr. Seuss stood impassively on my shelf, as always, and the staid Stanley Gibbons' *Commonwealth and British Empire Stamp Catalogue* seemed to glare at me with a challenge. Find her!

Macy and Walter, strangely, seemed unaltered over breakfast. Quiet. Reflective. Almost indeterminate. I finished my bowl of cornflakes before the milk turned its contents to mush, and I almost bounded up the stairs to get my backpack ready for school.

I didn't delay in the school grounds either in this new-found sense of purpose. Neither Leese nor, or course, Tom were present when I strode across the grassy playing ground, still wet from early morning dew. It was cold and winter would soon arrive, a formidable season on the central plains and prairie.

My intention was to go straight into the classroom before anyone was there. And that is what I did.

It was quiet. I was not used to being in the room alone. Its hushed atmosphere lent itself to looking at it anew, no longer as a field of learning but as a crime scene. For the first time I did not enter the room as a student.

Everything seemed to be as we had left it. Tidy, swept, orderly, and ready for the arrival of Mrs. Phillips. The faint scent of her perfume still hung in the air, like the light breeze of spring, for the duty of this vernal mistress to the wintry hibernation of childish minds was to waken them from their dulled consciousness. And it was a task she relished.

Tom's shelf at the back was quickly distinguished by its overflowing contents with papers half out of books and a pencil case pushed into a top corner where it had no business resting. Leese's was a picture of order, with everything arranged according to size, and geometrically laden with the requirements of learning. Mine was mostly empty.

The desks were aligned in straight rows, ready for straight backs and soles planted firmly on the ground. No books lay atop any desk. The only desk surface permitted any item was that of Mrs. Phillips, and then only what was strictly necessary and which could not be stored in the drawers or organized according to colour. The attendance folder was one of those items. It was not there.

I listened intently to hear any noises in the hall. All was silence. I shifted up to Mrs. Phillips' desk and tried the drawers. They were all locked. The surface was polished and clean, with no trace of chalk dust or pencil marks. What else should I have expected? I looked up to face the empty classroom. It was the first time I stood and really gazed from that spot. From her vantage point, on a slightly raised dais, nothing was hidden from her sight. Curious that I had always thought I could hide from her gaze. The attendance folder was slipped on top of the shelving unit that held our artifacts. It had no business being there. Except for standing on the dais, I would not have noticed it.

I could hear voices echo down the hall and I moved over to my desk and opened my backpack. I made an appearance as the eager student. This was an unusual role for me, and one that I had never knowingly played. Students were moving along to their classrooms and it was not long before the bell rang and my classroom filled. Tom was not there when the second bell rang. Nor, for that matter, was Mrs. Phillips. This was an occurrence we had never before experienced. We were all quite at loose ends. Tom ambled in some minutes late and stopped at the threshold. He hesitated. His was the role to be late. He had never, not even once, arrived when Mrs. Phillips was not present. Leese stared at him until he resolved to enter quietly.

The class remained curiously subdued as an ugly clock counted the silent minutes. Finally, as if nothing were at all amiss, Mrs. Phillips entered the classroom with short, deliberate steps and stood at her accustomed place, took us all in, and began as usual. For only the second time, she made no effort to take attendance, and after outlining the day's plan, launched breathlessly into the first lesson. It was not before mid-morning and the conclusion of a short break that she strode to the back of the room and removed the attendance folder from the top of the shelf and returned it to its precise place, the top right-hand corner of her desk. Never once did she open it. The day unwound without any other disturbance. We all left precisely as the concluding bell rang. As did Mrs. Phillips.

In the playground after school, Tom and Leese caught up with me. It was their first chance to discuss the recent events now that the first flush of excitement had subsided. For my part, I was waiting for a decent interval before going back into the classroom, just long enough to be sure it was emptied of all possible stragglers. I hardly took in Tom's and Leese's comments and questions. Yes. No. Maybe so. Finally, I interrupted Leese mid-sentence by wordlessly turning and striding back to the classroom. Her mouth hung open, unused to being ignored. "Where are you going?" But I just continued walking.

It seemed unlikely that the stamp had simply slipped out of place and was lost. There were too many eyes and there was too much interest when I was showing off my discovery for it just to have been misplaced without notice. It had to have been deliberate. It could have been any of my classmates, but that seemed unlikely. They would not have had the presence of mind to perform a sleight of hand so brazenly. Children, after all, by and large, are not good thieves. They have not yet learned to completely ignore a basic sense of justice, having themselves suffered repeated little injustices from their place amongst the entirely powerless. They are still inflamed with the sense of wrong, even if they can do nothing about it. It takes the superior ratiocinations of adults to blunt the sword of justice, and sheath it in a scabbard of tin excuses. Even if I found some of my students "disagreeable," to use Ms. Burnett's word from *The Secret Garden*, I don't think I would have accused any of them of trying to rob me. So who? Who would try to cheat me out of my great-grandfather's careful trust?

Mr. Carruthers would value the stamp as it was, knowing that its worth resided in its rarity. He could appreciate the joys of collecting abstracted from the monetary value of the pieces that composed the collection itself. It was the wonder of scarcity that thrilled him. His weakness was his enthusiasm.

Mrs. Phillips was more calculating. Her strength lay in the methodical way she approached everything. It was hard to imagine her exhibiting any spontaneity at any time for any matter. Order. Regularity. Predictability. These were her virtues. They were also her weakness. She could face disorder, inconsistency, and the capricious only by casting a net over them and catching them into a web of imposed stability.

I was just on the threshold of the school's institutional doors that simultaneously served to keep some in and some out, when I noticed a plod of movement in my peripheral vision. I turned my head to see Mr. Carruthers striding — or so it would have been called if his legs had been longer — down the sidewalk away from the main entrance to the school. With his battered briefcase locked in his hand, he was stiffly motionless as his body worked his legs, and his neck projected slightly forward with determination. He was intent on some business and took no notice of me, even if his thick lenses would have been able to detect me from his peripheral vision. I turned to Leese and Tom quickly and jerked my head in the direction of Mr. Carruthers. They hadn't noticed him, and as I slipped over the threshold, I could just barely hear Tom exclaim, "Hey, isn't that...?" I hoped Mr. Carruthers hadn't heard, but he was quite far off and proceeded apace without hesitation.

I went down the hall and into the classroom. It wasn't locked and there were probably some of the staff still around, but I couldn't hear anyone. Leese and Tom came up behind me and remained silent. Better for everyone if we entered and left unseen and unnoticed.

The room was quiet but not put in order. Mrs. Phillips had also left in a hurry. She normally would have stayed behind to line up the desks, remove stray books and waylaid pencils, and generally get her classroom ready for the next day. She must have had pressing business today that took her out of the class straight after the bell had rung.

I glanced briefly around the room. The attendance folder was on her desk, but it was not in its usual spot. It was displaced to the left. Mrs. Phillips had either been careless or distracted, which would have been unusual in itself, or else someone had rearranged the contents of the surface of her desk. I looked up and waited to hear any sounds. Leese and Tom just looked at me.

Leese remarked after a moment, "Doesn't she keep the attendance folder over there?" She pointed to the top right corner of the desk. "She forgot to take attendance, too." I nodded, pleased that Leese had noted the detail.

Tom shrugged his shoulders. If it wasn't of the wild kingdom, he paid little attention.

Not hearing any footsteps or voices approach in the hallway, I tried the desk drawers. They were all locked. As usual.

I opened the attendance folder. It was black and had pink, lined cards in each little slot, topped with the name of a student and on each line, in neat, studied script, a date and time for each truancy. I pulled out Tom's. His card was already working on the reverse side. Nothing was entered for today. Even Tom had been spared.

It would have been easy to slip a stamp behind one of the pink cards, a perfect ruse until the stamp could be removed, unseen, and secured elsewhere. Is this what she had done? Hid the stamp in front of everyone?

Then why was Mr. Carruthers just here? Had he contrived to smuggle the treasure? Was he just coming back to retrieve it from where he had hidden it all along? My strength lay in determining patterns, not in searching out missing elements or random actions or plumbing the motives of deceit in human beings. The pattern was clear. The attendance folder had never strayed from its rightful place on the top right-hand corner of Mrs. Phillips' desk until the day my queen went missing.

I pointed this out to Tom and Leese in whispered tones. I didn't want anyone hearing us and coming into the classroom to ask questions. I had enough questions of my own. I explained my theory to them and they nodded, thinking it over.

Tom glanced around the room. His skill lay in knowing what was out of place, in finding where the pattern was broken. His own approach to routine was simple: kill it with random acts of defiance. He balked at arriving on time, he had no organization in his school desk or in his back shelf, he had no order to his room. His whole destiny, it seemed, was to deliberately sink a black hole into the rational calculations of the cosmos. He took some satisfaction in the fact that today, for the first time, Mrs. Phillips had not straightened up the room before leaving. Even the blackboards had not been wiped clean. The last, frantic lesson was still written in white chalk, the usual firm letters of the teacher now bent forward uncharacteristically as if in a race to keep up with the thought that produced them, or the impatience of having to utter them.

Leese took delight in the motives of the human mind, plumbing the reasons for invention or war. She focused on Mrs. Phillips' desk. She tried the drawers again. They were still locked. She cast a look at the sides of the desk. Then she reached under the desk, sliding her hand along the bottom rail that joined each of the desk's legs. She stopped on the right side of the desk and tugged hard at something. She produced a key strapped with tape to the underside of the rail. Wordlessly, she held it up at eye level with a beaming grin on her face. "An organized person would hide a spare. She would never leave anything to chance."

Tom and I stood amazed. Leese glided the key into the locks and opened all the drawers. The ordered tools of our enlightenment appeared in coloured boxes neatly fitting into the spaces. Spare pencils and erasers, chalk and coloured markers. Everything. Sheets of paper, notepads. Everything we might forget to bring in our backpacks she had in her drawers. Anything she needed, too.

"Would she risk hiding it in here?" I asked. "If she was the one who took it..."

"Better here than at home. If anyone decided to search her home and found it there, it would prove she was guilty for sure." Leese scanned the room. "Better if it were left here. Then she could just say it had slipped, or been misplaced, or been swept somewhere. No one could actually *prove* that she *intended* to steal it." It was a good point.

The drawers did not turn up my stamp. We locked them all, replaced the key carefully, and noiselessly left the building.

Walter and Macy looked tired when they came home and we spoke little over supper. My dad said he hadn't heard anything from the police yet. He didn't ask me if I had come up with anything new. An eleven-year-old would not. Even if he were a giant. I went up to my room to finish some homework, which provided a surprisingly welcome diversion for my thoughts. The math exercises added up, as they should. But Dr. Seuss' coloured fish seemed to stare at me, speaking and pointing fins, which they should not. And Captain America just gazed vacantly at the ceiling, useless in the face of a real crisis.

Where would one hide a stolen stamp in a classroom full of childhood activity? It was the question I could not answer, for there was no pattern to the action. It did not fit.

The next morning began as all the others. The excitement of the last days was over for most of my classmates, and for my teacher, too, it seemed. Tom turned up on time, though, and Leese was reprimanded for inattention. I did my best not to attract notice and it worked. We were wrapping up the day with our half hour of hobbies and no one asked me a single question about the lost stamp. I had brought other stamps to look at as well as Stanley Gibbons' catalogue to make it look like I was carrying on as normal.

"Hey!" someone cried out from the back of the room. We all looked around. It was Leese, who stood incredulous by her shelf, staring at her ordered books. Only it wasn't the books she was looking at. She reached a few shelves down and pinched something between her fingers firmly but delicately, raising it up to inspect it. It was my stamp. The queen had been ransomed.

I rushed up to Leese and looked closely at the tiny square, then I looked up at Mrs. Phillips, who had a strange expression on her lips. It wasn't astonishment, but more like relief. She let out a short burst of air from her mouth, and with great strides arrived beside Leese.

"I knew it must be around. And here it is!" Some of my classmates came up too. "Finally." She took the stamp from Leese, holding it gently at the edges as she transferred it to me. "Now the riddle is solved, and we can put it behind us," she said with a slight nod of the head and a stiffening of her spine.

I put the Penny Black into my catalogue with the other stamps. But I did not want to risk another loss, so I asked to call my father. After all the students had left, he arrived. Mrs. Phillips had finished tidying up the classroom and waited. She explained where and how it had been found.

With the mystery solved, we drove to the bank to lock the Penny Black in a safety deposit box. This was not my choice. I would have preferred to take it home so I could examine it better, but I knew Walter would never go for it. Sitting in the car on the way to the bank, I looked at my great-grandfather's gift again. It stared up at me with the haughty expression I had first recognized. The colouring was good and the image looked true, but it just didn't "feel" right. The little raised lines caused by the press of the classic laid paper were there. And then it struck me. The century-old gum on the back, which had worn and deteriorated over such a long time, was missing. Someone had gone to a lot a trouble to get the image just right, and the paper just right. But replicating the gum had failed.

I didn't say anything. What was the point? Everyone was so relieved at the discovery that no one would have listened.

CHAPTER EIGHT

The problem was who to tell. Someone had gone through a lot of trouble very quickly to create a forgery. They couldn't have gotten everything right, I supposed, in such a short time. And they probably calculated that it would be enough to fool an eleven-year-old, at least long enough to allow them to dispose of the real stamp before the forgery was discovered. Then there was the question of who had done it and how they had placed the forged bit of paper in a place to be seen, but yet appear as if it had slipped there by accident. So far, their strategy had worked. The found stamp was safely in a safety deposit box. Walter had come to take it. There was no plan to do anything with the stamp for the moment, just relief that it had been reclaimed. Mr. Carruthers had been informed that the valuable stamp was found; the school had called him right away. Everyone seemed satisfied. The police, too, had closed their case.

I sat on my bed that evening, staring at the gnostic Seuss, awaiting wisdom:

From there to here
from here to there
funny things are everywhere!

Mr. Carruthers had been at the school the day before, right after classes were ended. Mrs. Phillips had briefly become so disoriented as to make a late appearance and once again forget to take attendance. Tom, of course, was the immediate beneficiary, but what was the reason for her distraction? Until now she had been always an imperviable barrier against any human emotion, a vanguard militant stolidly dedicated to the dull and the routine, a she-warrior laying siege against the tacit and immoveable resistance of the walled minds of weak and feckless school children. She imposed order where chaos, as if by default, strove to waste the progeny of suburban decay.

Curious. Walter and Macy, Mrs. Phillips, even Mr. Carruthers in his Edwardian subterfuge, had always been so much furniture in the varied rooms of my daily life. Home. School. Hobby. These were voids I passed through each day in a dwelling that was not of my own design. I had paid so little attention to the contents of my life. It was safe and secure like a mini fortress. Macy and Walter made it so. Mrs. Phillips raised the perimeter of the stockade and erected the central keep from which I could peer out onto the hostile landscape high up and locked in. Mr. Carruthers provided a ready distraction to amuse and divert and veil the fact that adventure was kept at bay and defined within the strict mathematical limits that quantified the solution to every one of life's conundrums. These people were as so many objects in my life, present there for my security, edification, and diversion. I saw them every day, yet without once having truly looked at them.

One fish
Two fish
Red fish
Blue fish.

But Dr. Seuss gave me no enlightenment.

I would have to decide what to do with the help of Tom and Leese. Together we would plot a counter siege. We huddled in a windy corner of the schoolyard once the demands of the school day had released us.

It was easier to convince Leese that something was truly amiss. She was always invigorated by the prospect of every human fall which purpled the map of her world. Heroism and vice, after all, were the axes around which spun the globe of human history. Tom was infuriatingly dull and unmoved. He was guided by the conviction that natural forces should be left to follow their inherent destinies, that justice was produced by the clash of irresistible tendencies seeking ever and again a perfect stasis. And me? I had been goaded at last from the complacency that every problem could be solved by the discovery of an adequate mathematical formula. Base human calculation, not wistful algorithms, were the arms alone with which victory could be purchased.

Tom was brought around although he remained, at heart, unconvinced. Leese stood at the ready. All we needed was a strategy.

But we were eleven years old, and even a giant, a troll, and an aspiring naturalist, at that age, had limits. Nevertheless, our youth was our strength. We did not yet calculate as did the adults that furnished our world, and what was otherwise considered a deficiency could yet be marshalled to our advantage. The question was how.

Mrs. Phillips would need more thought because, although she was a fixed spot on the morning horizon of our days, she remained a dark spot nevertheless, inscrutable in her regularity. And then she vanished with equal regularity each afternoon crepuscule into another horizon that did not belong to us. Mr. Carruthers, on the other hand, although a recent acquaintance, was somewhat more known, at least to me. He had inspired in me something akin to interest in an otherwise ordinary and thoughtless task. And what was more, he was the cause of bringing me into contact with a distant and silent relative, and the peculiar feeling that I had been waited for.

Tom, Leese and I decided that I should visit Mr. Carruthers to discuss the events of the days and report back all the details so that, together, Tom, Leese, and I could cull the results and plan the next move.

I knew the bus route well by now, and, again, because of my outgrown size, I caused little stir that a child was left to board public transit or wander the streets alone. No one took a second glance at me. I stood across the street, looking into the shop that stood one step up from the sidewalk. The dusty windows reflected the low glare of a late fall sun, but there seemed to be no movement within. I rehearsed what I should say. How much should I hint that I suspected a forgery and remained convinced of theft? How to broach the subject of his curious appearance at the school after hours the day before the finding of the copy? If he had truly stolen the stamp, he might possibly seek corroborating evidence that I still suspected nothing in him, and so reassure himself that he had yet a little allowance of time to complete the robbery and hide his involvement. How should I react? Walter and Macy had never had the least trouble detecting a lie — not that they always called me out on it. But I knew they knew. So, I practiced what I thought would be an immoveable, inscrutable face. I puffed my cheeks slightly so they were full, and studiously avoided furrowing my brow. A wrinkled brow or any sudden sucking in of the cheeks would, I thought, give myself away. I still had something of a baby face, so it wasn't hard, and, as an afterthought, I prepared to keep my eyes open and prevent myself from unexpected blinking. Steeling my intention not to give anything away by my look or bearing from the one person I had recently taken as my mentor, I crossed the street and turned the rusty door handle.

The bell on the faded red ribbon tinkled and tapped on the oval window of Carruthers' Collectors Stamps as I entered the streaming dusty light. The same varnished and patinated oak surrounded me and the waft of dusty paper filled my nostrils. It was a comforting smell which threatened to lure me into a spirit of confidentiality, but I drew back my shoulders and lifted my chin to resist the temptation. I was here on a clandestine and pressing errand and so had to be mindful of traps laid for the unwary. A sense of purpose stiffened my back.

Mr. Carruthers appeared out of the dust when I turned from looking out onto the street back to the glass case where I had seen him that first day we met.

This time he did not seem conjured before me. Rather, he stood bent over the framed wooden case facing the door. He had neither heard the tinkle of the bell as I entered nor seen me glide up to him. He was intent on a book in front of him. I could not tell what it was, but his finger was pointing to a picture of the Penny Black and his thoughts were engrossed with some private matter. I wondered if he had ever, in his life, a public thought to manifest. I continued to stare down at him, without moving, until he noticed I was there. I somehow sensed that this would be to my advantage. It was usually he who caught his clients unawares.

"Ahhhh," he wheezed. And then, "Ivan." I simply continued to look at him. I had startled him and it was a sensation he was not used to. He took his finger from the page, looked from me back down to the book, but made no attempt to hide it.

"Good news, Ivan. Good news."

"Yes, Mr. Carruthers," I replied. "My father has locked the stamp up in the safety deposit box."

"To be sure," he said, regaining his accustomed manner of speaking. "It should be safe there."

"Surely."

There was silence. I didn't quite know how to proceed. No diversionary techniques came to mind, as the main point we had in common now was my lost stamp and it was impossible to speak of anything else.

"Do you have any further information about the history of the Penny Black?"

"No, not really. Yours is a unique find, and a stamp in unusually good condition. Mint, it seems."

We went over again the curious way in which I had found it. Speaking out loud, I was struck again by the prescience of my ancestor. Why had he so curiously hidden it? He obviously knew that he had something of note, maybe even of worth. Had he speculated that its worth would increase in time if it lay hidden for longer? Who could guess his thoughts? Maybe they didn't have safety deposit boxes back then and this was his best bet for safekeeping. Maybe it was his Dr. Seuss ruse of a hundred years ago.

A slight smile lifted the ends of Mr. Carruthers' mouth. It was not unpleasant. Could he have created the forgery so quickly? Who else would have known the minute details of the image that needed to be replicated and the type of paper that needed to be used? Maybe he had old sheets of paper in his back stockroom? Perhaps this wasn't his first forgery.

That *was* an unpleasant thought. The idea of having been lulled into complacency so that a master criminal could use my innocence to his advantage.

I omitted the Dr. Seuss ruse in my recapitulation of the discovery to Mr. Carruthers.

"So now you have her back."

I hesitated. Here was the door open. How to push through it and keep my innocence intact?

"Yes."

"And how has Mrs., ahhh… Phillips, I believe… received the news?"

I hesitated, recalling again her face when she pinched the stamp from Leese's grasp. "Relieved, I think."

"I should think so," was all he said, but he seemed to stare more intently into my face. I turned away quickly for a moment, but I did my best neither to suck in my cheeks nor blow out my breath. And I made sure I did not blink my eyes.

"And so you are satisfied? You are content?"

"Yes, I suppose." I hesitated again. I was trying to give him a clue that I had not been quite deceived, even if I could say that the discovery brought some satisfaction.

"And now what do you propose to do?"

"I'm not sure. I was hoping you might have some ideas." I stared back, unblinking, at Mr. Carruthers, who continued to scrutinize me a little too intently.

"To be sure. To be sure." He glanced down at the book. "I should need some time to think. It is not so easy to dispose of such a thing."

"I suppose not."

"One would have to contact various… ah… interested parties. It is not likely that it would be put to public offer."

"Are there buyers you know who would be interested?"

He smiled. "Certainly. Greatly interested, I should think. But first the stamp must be authenticated, you see. To make sure it is not a forgery," he broke off.

I said nothing, trying not to blink and suck in my cheeks.

"Sometimes forgeries come on the market." He stared at me. "They can be very cleverly done. Very difficult to detect."

"And how can you make a forgery of such an old thing?"

"It requires a determined mind. A criminal mind. It requires extensive knowledge of the true item so that it can be replicated in all its detail. It requires knowledge, too, of the history of that particular stamp." He stopped for a moment. "Each stamp has had a life of its own. It's seen its little parcel of the world that we cannot see. It's travelled. It's been handled, it's been in cargo bags, on trains or ships; it's been stamped — if it was used — and kept in drawers, touched by postmen, drawn in wagons behind horses. A stamp, you see, Ivan, has its own history."

He stared at me. I stared back.

"It is not an easy thing to replicate that history."

Mr. Carruthers' world was opening to me. The fascination, the obsession, really. A stamp represented to him more than a prepaid means of exchange. It represented a window into our lives, the lives that have been lived. The interests and individual persons who desired to reach out to others through letters, through words that described their own lives and loves and loss. It was a way to touch the past, those who had lived; it was a thread that bound us to them.

How great was Mr. Carruthers' obsession, I wondered? What wouldn't he do to put his finger on a page of the past? Clearly, it was not the monetary value, the investment, that drove him each day into his dusty shop that filtered the light of today, refracting it into a gaze upon the past. There was an imponderable motive to his life's work, a motive that he could only rarely share.

"It is not much, a stamp. Any yet it carries with it more than it can say."

It seemed appropriate to say nothing.

He looked back down at his book and put his finger over the face of the black queen. He stared for a moment, and without looking up, he said, "I will have to see the stamp again before anything can be decided."

I mentioned that I would speak to my father and then see what could be done. He simply nodded. He seemed a little sad.

"Yes. Well, Ivan. You will let me know what happens next, won't you?"

"Certainly, Mr. Carruthers." And there being nothing more to say, I turned towards the door and walked through shafts of dusty light. I heard the tinkle of the bell and the click of the door as I shut it behind me, without looking back.

Walking slowly to the bus stop, a confusion of conclusions ran through my mind. No one else could have the knowledge and perhaps the means to make a forgery so quickly and convincingly in such a short time. Yet forging a stamp seemed like it would be to Mr. Carruthers a treason against… what? History? The lives that had touched the printed image? It required a criminal mind, he had said.

I had a feeling the visit was a failure. I had gained no insight into what had been done or the motives for the doing. As a child, one is told not to lie or steal or cheat. These seem the summit of dishonest and criminal intent. One knows they happen, but only in small things. A stolen cookie, a lie to hide one's negligence, an answer cheated out of fear. But one has no experience of a big lie, a grown up lie. Yet they happen, of course. Someone does it. The question was, do they get away with it?

CHAPTER NINE

The bus ride home unfolded in slow motion. I felt dejected. I wasn't sure what I had accomplished. Opening the front door of our suburban house, I stopped on the threshold, embraced by the familiar and inviting spices that simmered in Macy's roast beef, chasing away the faint odour of rotting leaves and the musty earth that yielded its dead just before the frozen winter entombed all life. Macy was in the kitchen and Walter stood looking out the window by her side, suspended in mid-action. Neither heard me enter. I stood looking at them for a moment before making a small noise to alert them to my presence, but not to startle them. They smiled.

"Supper's almost ready," Walter assured.

I put my things up in my room, for once putting everything away carefully and not just throwing my bag by the bed. I sat on the edge of the bed and stared around my room. It was a child's room. What else would it be? A two-dimensional super-hero laying inert upon my bed, remnants of plush toys, those silent companions who until now had always thrown themselves into my plans. Human beings had always been too complicated to enlist in my strategies, as they always insisted on their own reasons for what they did. Stuffed bears don't have to worry about motives; they are in it only for the game and never have to suffer the consequences of other people's choices. That's why they make more willing accomplices than human beings, I thought. Action heroes, for their part, are of more limited use than bears because heroes are always trying to save the world. They're way too serious to simply enjoy the game. An imaginary world, after all, opens a door to excitement when life is otherwise dull and monotonous. Does one invent a dull world when excitement overtakes life? Pretend danger is still circumscribed by an ordered day. What of real danger?

I had never had reason to distrust anyone in my whole life. Until that moment everyone around me had been colluding to keep me honest, but now a seemingly impenetrable wall had been pierced by a silent mortar shell, and life was turning on its head.

I came down to the dining room where we always ate our evening meal.

"Mr. Carruthers called..." Macy opened. Does a counterfeiter and a thief call your mom? "He says you were down to see him."

"Yes, I was."

"Did you tell him the stamp is safe again?"

"Yes, I did."

"He must have been pleased."

I hesitated, looking down at my plate. "Yes." And then, "Relieved."

"I should think he would be. As were we...."

And so it seemed everything was all right with the world.

Only it wasn't. I had a great-grandfather who was still very disappointed and would like some answers.

The next day, I met up with Tom and Leese. They were of no help. We still had no strategy. No strategy meant I did not have a way to reclaim my great-grandfather's legacy. It meant someone else had succeeded in stealing it. It meant someone else was lying. Not only had they taken it, they had quickly concocted a plan to distract attention and buy time, paid for in the currency of my innocence. But that was where their mistake lay. I had not been duped. Still, I didn't yet have a plan to restore justice and redeem my ancestor's trust in me. One thing I had concluded however:

the fact that they thought I had been fooled could work to my advantage. It might make them less cautious and I needed to find a way to leverage their overestimation of my naiveté. For the moment it was my only tool and it desperately needed to be reinforced.

When Mrs. Phillips asked me if my father had delivered the stamp into the bank's safety deposit box, I replied that he certainly had. And I smiled, trying to look pleased. She seemed to smile her pleasure back. But reading the meaning behind a smile on Mrs. Phillips' face had never been an easy task, since "happy" and "pleased" were not adjectives one associated frequently with her demeanour. She chattered noisily down the hallway on her way to lunch, clucking about an exotic holiday she had long dreamed of taking and thought now might be realized: a slow cruise winding listlessly through little-inhabited islands of ancient civilization.

For my part, I was marooned on an unfamiliar and foreign shore, still lost as to what direction to follow, but it struck me that my time could best be spent by simple observation. My strength was recognizing patterns and regularity, a calculated predictability and certainty. The mathematics of life. Mrs. Phillips was anything if not regularity itself, and aside from a slight change in demeanour today, she had resumed her patterned habits. I supposed that a teacher's strength was one that rested on methodical preparation. A student like me might allow himself to show up for a class with little forethought and his homework perfunctorily complete, but it was a teacher's task to draw out expected results and calculable outcomes from the woolly heads of youth. This required preparation in order to mould the activities of others into the predetermined pattern, to push their ill-prepared efforts into formulaic conclusions. Or so it seemed from my end of the teaching equation. Tom may have been quite prepared to tease the teacher to revise the formula for results, and Leese to meditate on the greater motivations of results-oriented activity, but my strength lay in anticipating the formula and completing it with as little disruption to my day as possible, while at the same time eliciting the least notice. In other words, I liked to disappear behind the standard approach to any problem. Singularity was the enemy of my strategy. And so, by the end of the day when we finally resumed our hobby activities, not one other student in the room asked me about the stamp that had been lost and found. All was as it had been. So all was as it should be.

But, of course, it wasn't.

My world was peopled with actors who entered upon the stage of my life and then disappeared. Mrs. Phillips appeared each morning, Monday to Friday, regular as the ugly clock on the classroom wall that told time in bold and clear numbers. Then she disappeared when I closed the school door behind me. Like a paper cut-out, she had no dimension other than the extension that walked into my life in the morning and walked out each late afternoon. As I watched her chatter volubly to the other teachers in the hall again at the end of class, it finally struck me that she probably lived a three-dimensional life, much like mine and Macy's and Walter's. The only three-dimensional people in my life were these two parents, and then only just. I had treated all of the actors as if they only existed by their contact with my own existence. This was hardly fair. And, in the flash of an instant, my own insignificance finally broke through the dull fogginess of my slow-dawning consciousness. In the face of these varied and fully dimensional lives that entered stage right and exited stage left in my life, my own activity seemed suddenly and alarmingly two-dimensional.

It was with a sense of incredulity, therefore, that I hesitatingly followed Mrs. Phillips as she strode down the hall. She entered the teachers' staff room and I hung around for a while. Leese and Tom had already left, as had the rest of the students from my class. A few lingered here and there in the halls, tying shoelaces, bending down for a drink of water at the fountain, or listlessly ambling about, as if waiting for a parent to fetch them. I adopted the listless gait of the ambling few. Eventually, Mrs. Phillips came out the door, dressed with coat and hat and rather elegant mauve gloves. The weather had turned and mornings were chilled. The dying afternoon sun refused to generate any warmth.

If I had given it any thought at all, I suppose I had always assumed that, like my parents, Mrs. Phillips would get into her car parked in the staff lot and go home to some other suburb where she could live a life undisturbed by her daily charges. But in fact, as I shifted up to the long, vertical window of the school door, I could see she crossed the playground and disappeared on foot down one of the neighbourhood streets. I decided to follow at a distance. I pulled my toque down over my forehead and lifted a quilted hood over my head. It was a bit much for the weather, but it concealed me better. Very soon I gained the street she had followed just in time to see her turn right into a perpendicular lane. Hidden by the row of replicated houses, I trotted down, a little concerned that I might lose sight of her. As I reached the corner I stopped, then proceeded slowly around the bend, searching out her silhouette, careful to remain unseen. I was surprised to see her enter a small house, not much different in shape, colour, and contour to all the houses along the street. I went slowly up the street until I could see the house number. Then, as I dared not go farther in case she might come out unexpectedly, I turned back to the school yard to find my own way home, still impressed by the revelation that Mrs. Phillips lived on after I went home, and probably had a life not much different from mine.

Having discovered that the people in my life pursued lives outside the time they spent in the theatre of my own life, I decided that it might be interesting to see what Mr. Carruthers had for a life beyond the dusty storefront of his shop of collectibles. So the next day, after school, I boarded a bus as it wound its way out of the grassy suburbs into the centre of town. For the first time, I looked about and realized that not everyone lived in a house away from town. There were large apartment blocks and, what I had never noticed before, an urban school. It was built of red brick, an unusual building material on the prairies. It had ornate doors. One side of the building had a stone lintel with "Boys" carved above the heavy wooden doors. It was echoed by a lintel on the opposite end with "Girls" carved atop. In between were large sash windows, painted white with multiple panes in each. It was unlike the crisp, grey-rendered walls of my suburban school with its grand expanses of clear glass that brought light in and kept winter snows out. The playground of this ancient school was small and lined by an old chain link fence, bowed here and there as if children had been thrown against it in bygone years to leave their imprint in the wire mesh. Life must have been unkinder when brick schools were built. But, then again, what did I know of my own life and times? Pretty much nothing, I realized. Wide steps led up to the front door glinting with quarter-paned windows that reflected red into the setting afternoon sun. Above the door was carved 1907, a very early building by local reckoning. Queen Victoria had died early in 1901 and would have looked very different from her image on the Penny Black, printed when she was still young and haughty.

Arriving finally at my bus stop, I alighted and slowly walked up the street towards the familiar glass door painted with ancient script marking Mr. Carruthers' shop. I had no idea what I was doing there. It was simple curiosity designed to gain some insight into the peculiar habits of Mr. Carruthers himself. I don't know if I had planned to go in, but as I hesitated on the curb about a half block away, I heard the faint tinkle of the bell on the faded red ribbon and saw a figure step down, out of the door of the shop. To my shock, it was Mrs. Phillips with the same mauve-coloured gloves as the day before. She did not look to the right or the left but adjusted her hat, and then walked up to a small but smart blue car parked along the sidewalk. I watched as she got in and drove away. It was nearing 5:00 p.m. and the winter evening was already advancing. The sun was glowing low on the horizon and the street lights flickered in the early dusk. I walked forward, and then I saw a hand reach up in the door window and hang a sign. "Closed." However, I knew the posted hours of the shop said it was open until 6:00 p.m. The lights of the store blinked and then it remained dark, darker than the street. I was curious to see what Mr. Carruthers would do, where he would go after he closed his store. I slipped down the back alley behind the row of old storefronts. I found a discreet spot where I would not be seen, but there was no movement whatsoever. It took me a moment to calculate which was the rear of Mr. Carruthers' store. It had a small garage and a fenced yard. Very soon a light on the second storey was turned on, and I noticed for the first time that it was a three-storey building, looking suspiciously like it had been built in the days of the wild west: sturdy but toppled with age. I waited for what seemed another age. A few other windows were lit from within and I was startled to conclude that Mr. Carruthers lived above his shop.

Returning home feeling, again, little enlightened by my contact with Mr. Carruthers and more confused than ever, my parents asked me where I had been. So I told them I had been to see Mr. Carruthers.

"Oh. And what did he have to say?"

"Not much." It wasn't a lie.

"Did he show you anything interesting?"

"Sort of." Again, it wasn't an untruth.

"Well, if he has other stamps he thinks would be good for your collection, tell him we'll buy them. At least, as long as they are not priceless." It was a lame attempt at humour, and its lameness was part of its appeal. I tried to show I appreciated it. But all I could think was that a forgery is not a priceless possession.

My parents' interest ended there, for which I was grateful. Walter and Macy had always been respectful of my independence even when I had not really asserted it. For them, the history of the lost and found stamp was over, relegated to a past anxious moment and coloured by a general sense of relief.

We ate our simple supper, which I hardly noticed, after which I went up to my room to finish homework and to avoid pursuing thoughts that led nowhere, and events in which I could trace no discernable pattern.

CHAPTER TEN

———◆◆◆———

Macy's voice from the hall awakened me the next morning as it had done every morning since I could remember, which was not a very long span of time. "So now what?" was the first thought that entered my awakening mind. It was not a question I felt comfortable with and it felt quite new. My activities had never been my own possession. I arose to the schedule set by another. I ate a breakfast prepared by another. I walked to a school that was built by another, to follow classes that were designed by another, there to produce results that were expected by others. What remained for myself of my own life was little indeed. A fantasy world between bouts of homework and supper.

So now what?

I didn't get up.

Macy was shuffling downstairs and Walter was tucked away at his morning ablutions. The sounds, so familiar, were somehow new.

It was not my habit to be called a second time. This was not accomplished out of any contempt for indolence, but out of a residual respect for my parents who needed to get their day going… and so needed to get mine going too. Indolence can be achieved even in the midst of an otherwise externally active life. It is a question of attitude rather than effort. I had been indolently busy for most of my life, keeping to the schedules of others.

"So now what?" This simple question confronted me with the need to engage in my own form of planning. But in order to plan, one needs an end, a goal, an object, and a purpose. These were, none of them, a strong point of reference in my daily activity. So the question made me uncomfortable. I stared at Captain America, wrapped around me, sprawled, dishevelled, and inert.

"So now what?"

The question continued to perplex me throughout the day. Winter had definitely arrived and the wind did not just chasten, it bit and drove, as only a great plain's wind can do. The walk to school numbed my cheeks, and my fingers thawed slowly in the classroom. A grey sky suppressed all mirth, and the routine seemed drudgery without respite. Even Leese was subdued, and Tom dull. Mrs. Phillips carried on with significant indifference, but she finally sighed in mid-afternoon as we prepared to bundle ourselves out the door with slow reluctance. The day brought no answer to my question. "Wait," it seemed to say. "Patience, endurance."

Without deliberation of any sort, I retraced my steps and found myself standing across from the house of Mrs. Phillips, alone. I could feel my eyelashes tickle beneath my eyebrows with an icy brush each time they blinked and opened again. No one was in the street. The windows of the house were darkened. The street, too, was colourless in early winter twilight. I walked to the end of the block and turned down a perpendicular street. A narrow and neglected alley gave out onto the sidewalk and I entered its gloom. Alleys are forgotten streets in prairie towns. Unkempt and overgrown. A no man's land where only garbage collection and electrical companies run their industrial vehicles, like green-grey tanks, close by but out of sight to the civilized suburban streets. Potholes and unrepaired fence boards. Chairs with amputated limbs and dressing tables with gaping rectangular wounds unfit for restoration indoors. Urban desolation. The underside of domestic charm.

The wind, nevertheless, was less biting here, and the silence more complete. I counted back the houses from the alley entranceway and stopped. Here too everything was in order, a sharp contrast to the jumbled and rejected world of her neighbours. Swept concrete leading into a freshly-painted garage and perfectly vertical fence boards that dared not lean or twist. When one looked straight on, the small gaps between the boards were insufficient to glean what lay beyond, but as I carried on walking, I looked back, and there was one spot where the rear garden revealed itself through the narrow interstices. The mind stitched the patterns together, and a clear view was gained.

It was a modest garden. The snow had held off until now, so the depressing death of winter was unblanketed. A tall, columnar aspen shot to the sky with empty limbs, grey, crooked, and spindly. Leafless shrubs hunkered along the neighbour's wall. Impossible to tell which type of dwarf trees they were now their leaves were gone and they had been pruned severely back. And there was not a leaf upon the ground anywhere. Vegetable beds had been raided and the earth turned against the elements in horizontal furrows. The grass ceased to give colour. It was the twilight hue of domestic straw.

In a corner, backing onto the far side of the garage, was a small and perfectly-formed garden shed. It leaned for support against the wall. Walking back, I thrust my head forward, with an eye spying through the vertical gap in the fence. There was a padlock, but the padlock was not closed and the metal clasp was unlatched. I looked again around the garden without turning my head when suddenly Mrs. Phillips charged out from the shed. I hadn't heard her at all. Nor, thankfully, had she heard me. I managed to stifle an instinct to gasp in surprise or fright. It would certainly be an awkward thing to have to explain my presence, an eye pressed against the interstice between two fence boards, and I would have been utterly unconvincing.

She was carrying a small, metal case, flashing even under the grey clouds. She clutched it peculiarly with two hands folded over the edge. It could not have been more than twenty centimetres in length and somewhat narrower in width. But it did not look new. Rather, it appeared well looked after but old. Now, in what was left of the daylight, she deftly opened the case and peered intently at the contents. I could see nothing. She was concentrating and it occurred to me that she would not see me, partly because I remained hidden behind the fence, but mostly because she would not be expecting anyone to be peering through. The fear that had arisen with my first shock of surprise left me, strangely, and so I, too, peered intently. Observation was the only tool left me against those who had deprived me of my inheritance, and so I tried to observe carefully. I was unsuccessful. Mrs. Phillips snapped the box shut with a nod of her head and, turning deliberately, she retreated to her back door. She disappeared out of the frosty early evening, and a light blinked from within.

It could have been anything, of course. But I knew that once winter had really and truly set in on the prairies, there was no need and no reason to retrieve anything from a garden shed. The garden would lay dormant for months. So, it seemed to me, the pattern was broken. Mrs. Phillips had taken orderly care to see that her garden was carefully prepared for the winter. Not a leaf on the ground. No residual works to accomplish hurriedly on the first day when winter announced its arrival. No reason to enter a garden shed when the garden lay dead already. Stealing into the shed in such circumstances was irregular.

Relieved that I had not been discovered, I was relieved also that snow had not yet fallen to betray my presence with confused footprints pointing in every direction. Care and forethought to action would be required of me in the future.

I was acquiring a series of discoveries that I could share with no one. At least, not yet. Suspicions are awkward, intangible things: impossible to refute because impossible to prove. For some, they can be a morose signal to give up; but for others, they can be an inducement to further inquiry. I wanted to investigate further. But where to look? And for what?

The next day I mentioned to Tom and Leese that I would be going down to Mr. Carruthers' store to seek out more stamps for my collection. And, I vaguely thought, to create at least the illusion of furthering my hobby. Perhaps through the subterfuge of such a visit, I might find more threads that would weave together a new pattern and show up a clearer image of what needed to be done next.

Tom and Leese decided to tag along, "If that's okay," Leese added, after excitedly saying that she'd like to come with me. She was looking at me now a little hesitantly. The tone of her voice was a higher pitch than usual and her words ran together very slightly, like she was trying without success to suppress an eagerness. Their brief encounter during show and tell with the patron of my collection, followed by the shock of loss, the relief of recovery, and then my intimations of theft, had rustled a breeze of curiosity. For both of them, it was an adventure that had happened to someone else, but they were game to enter something which promised excitement. We all boarded the bus together. While I could not be alone with my thoughts in the company of friends, I still made the effort to observe the world outside the window as we were thrown haltingly from the suburb into the quiet side-street of the city.

Leese, in particular, was paying attention to the ordinary lives we passed and occasionally remarked on this or that, playing in her imagination a strange game of guesswork and deduction. A woolen hat suggested — in her mind — travel to an informal meeting. Leather gloves, the work of a lawyer or accountant. Impractical shoes, a habit of distraction and unpreparedness. I looked down at my own feet, shod thoughtlessly with a pair of neglected and abused running shoes.

As we jumped from the bus and took the short walk through a bracing wind to the door of the specialized emporium, we remained silent. I tried to align my motives and my thoughts but was finding the task rather difficult as it was unhabitual. Once inside, the silence amongst us hung on as Leese scanned the store, tracing a slow arc with her neck and head. Tom squinted in the dusty light and looked back out the window into the street, seemingly to note the immediate contrast without and within.

There was little enough on display, as usual. Whether this was by design or simply the result of a knowledgeable clientele which had no need to browse, I could not decide. Either way, it was a message. Enter here with seriousness and commitment. And if you must ask a question, let it not be random, but informed and considered. It was expected that you had done your research before you tinkled the bell on the door's ribbon to disturb the owner. He would not waste your time, and he anticipated the same courtesy in return.

It was not encouraging, as I had no set purpose to my visit.

"Ivan." It was spoken as a form of greeting, but without inflection of any kind. Mr. Carruthers had performed his trick again, appearing behind the glass case while we were strangely distracted by the sparse contents of the store.

"I see you have brought your friends. May I inquire of their names?"

"Certainly." Normally such a reply would have been awkward. "Lisa Troll and Thomas Andrew." Leese and Tom stared at me. Tom had a slight smile at the corners of his mouth but was prudent enough to refrain from comment.

"Very nice to meet you."

Leese and Tom murmured indistinct replies.

"Are you also interested in philately?"

Silence. I whispered "stamp-collecting" to them with an apologetic cough.

"No," said Tom, reasserting himself. "I tried paper-making for our hobby class at school, but I'm thinking of doing something else."

"Ahhh, yes. I recall. The day of show and tell,'" Mr. Carruthers said, looking at me rather than Tom. "Paper-making has a fine history and is not without its own interest and merits. It has been the conveyance of human industry and wisdom for millennia."

Tom was silent again.

"And I was examining old documents," Leese pushed in. "I liked the wax seals, too."

"Yes, I recall that too. Records of human decisions, that's what documents are," Mr. Carruthers added with a smile. I was not sure that I had ever seen him exactly *smile* before. It was genuine, which made it seem a bit odd. Adults frequently smile at children, but children just as frequently do not know why.

"We make many decisions in a lifetime, even in a day," Mr. Carruthers continued. "But how many of these do we commit to paper, and to pen and ink? Paper is the conveyance of human thought; pen and ink — and wax seals — the pledge and guarantee of its significance. A document is meant to speak to others, not to ourselves. It is meant to speak of our intentions, of our purpose, of the things that are important to us and which we esteem worthy to transcend our own isolation. Documents speak when our own voice falls silent."

Leese and Tom were stunned into bashful silence. Even Mrs. Phillips did not speak like this to us.

"…and stamps?" I asked.

Mr. Carruthers removed his glance now from Tom and Leese and seemed to fasten it on me. His eyes, enlarged and benign through his thick lenses, cleared a path through the dust to gaze at me. He reciprocated our silence for a moment. His thoughts settled, and then, "…and stamps? Stamps take our messages around the world. They ensure our thoughts will be read by others beyond the borders of our home or town or country. How, after all, are our decisions to take effect if we have no means to carry them forward? We can preserve them for ourselves, of course. But don't we need to execute our decisions for them to change the world?" He stopped. "Even if it is only the world of our own family strewn across the land or the continent?"

Here we had reached a limit. Tom looked back through the store windows. Leese, if I could have found the phrase at that time, seemed to be enveloped in a sort of rapture.

A thought came into my head.

"I was wondering if you might have some other stamps from around the time of the Penny Black, or even some time afterwards, maybe. I could compare them. They might help us understand why the Penny Black is so valuable."

Mr. Carruthers continued to gaze at me. A satisfaction was in his eyes.

"Context," was all he replied. "Absolutely right, Ivan. To understand the importance of any document," here he looked at Leese, "one needs to understand its situation within the context of similar documents of its own time, and then to consider how it had changed from those that went before, and how those that followed, in turn, changed and developed. That is the first way we need to 'situate' that which we have in order to understand its significance." Mr. Carruthers glanced over at Tom who was surveying the catalogues on the shelves. "And not just the picture or the words, but the material on which the words are crafted. They too give us context and the state of human innovation and ingenuity that underlie human decisions." He stopped. "All of these things — words, paper, ink, and seals — give us clues. Clues to the thoughts of the men and women of that time."

Again, he stopped. "I have been looking through some new stamps that someone just dropped off, requesting an appraisal. I haven't yet had a chance to valuate them but there are perhaps a few that might be useful.

They are from the British colonies. Nothing so famous or valuable as what you have," he hesitated, "but they might provide some useful comparisons."

Mr. Carruthers disappeared in the dusty air for a moment and reappeared. He placed a metal box on the counter and I stared at it. A metal case, shiny even in the dim light, but not new. In fact, the one I had seen just yesterday. "As I said, I have only just received this, but a quick examination of its contents shows one or two that might do." He picked a stamp marked "Gambia" along the top, with the picture, not of a queen, but of a king. A second one had an elaborate engraving of a sort of temple I had once seen, like the Taj Mahal. "India. The engraving is particularly fine. You can compare the technique with the Penny Black and note the improvements in the artwork." He examined the image more closely. "A great poet, William Butler Yeats, once said that the art and images on postage stamps and coins are 'the silent ambassadors on national taste.'"

He looked again more closely and said under his breath:

> There is nobody wise enough
> To find out all that is in it,
> For he would be thinking of love
> Till the stars had run away
> And the shadows eaten the moon.
> Ah, penny, brown penny, brown penny,
> One cannot begin it too soon.

"That's one of his poems. About casting a penny in a fountain and wishing for love."

Leese leaned in, captured on a swell of feeling. Tom remained immoveable in the face of romance. I was just embarrassed. Wishing wells and love were not the primary themes of comic book action stories or Dr. Seuss rhymes, even if they were already pulling somewhere at the periphery of my consciousness by that age.

"I think you should take these two," and Mr. Carruthers pushed them towards me so I could look more closely, but I kept looking back to the metal box.

"Are there any others in there?" There were, and he turned the box over to me so I could sift through the contents. I made a pretense of picking out one or two for closer inspection, without any real idea what I was looking for. There were quite a few, perhaps a hundred stamps or more, but as far as I could see none dated before about 1935. Most were British colonial with monarchs and architectural showpieces printed on them. There was a consistency, as far as I could tell, an interest in a particular theme and time.

I tried to examine the box itself and closed it to examine the lid. It was solid but very light with a small clasp on the front. It bore scratches at the clasp where, I supposed, a small lock might have caused the damage. Mr. Carruthers peered on, but he did not seem to be surprised by my investigations. The distracted curiosity of a boy. Which was true enough, although the cause of the curiosity could not be known to him.

In the end, I followed his suggestions and he said he would valuate them and let me know the cost. If it was too much, I could exchange them for others. He was certain there would be others that would serve my purpose. He appeared pleased to be my tutor.

Leaving the store, Tom was perplexed. Leese seemed to glow. I felt unnerved.

Leese went on for some time during the ride back to the suburbs about the marvels of the store and Mr. Carruthers. I made appropriate sounds when… appropriate. Tom remained silent.

CHAPTER ELEVEN

I found myself lying on my bed staring upward. Dr. Seuss lay open beside me but he had given up his treasure. No fishes in the sea. I had turned the bed cover over so that Captain America was no longer visible; he irked me now. I impatiently tapped my right foot in the air, striking nothing. I had absolutely no idea what to do next, nor what to do at all. An overwhelming angry frustration enveloped me for the first time. There must be something I should do, but I could not conceive what it must be. Something logical. Something reasonable. But what is the measure of reason at eleven? Dr. Seuss was silent. One-two-three, red and blue, sad and good, and very, very bad.

Who hides a stamp collection in a garden shed? Who brings it in to sell all at once when the one item of great value suddenly appears? Where is the logic in that?

No more questions!

I sat up suddenly and kicked at an invisible foe. But it brought me no relief.

Do something!

I thumped down the stairs… one-foot, two-foot, first-foot, blue-foot… thump thump thump. Walter and Macy were in the kitchen preparing supper. Walter was brandishing a knife, and he lifted it as I came in. It went down. Thwump.

I sat at the table and scowled. At least, I presume it was a scowl. I had read about scowls. I wasn't sure. I swung one foot violently and let the heel stick to the floor while I struck the table with the base of my two palms. Walter hesitated in mid-air, glancing at me from the corner of his eye before he came down on the bone of a wretched beast. Macy turned a quarter so that the corner of her eye met the corner of his, and she arched an eyebrow. It was a three-way conversation of sorts, best left suspended in the air between us. Not all talk in our house was a conversation. I pulled my palms to the edge of the table with a slow rasping that satisfied my scowl. Walter sliced an onion.

"Mr. Carruthers called. He says you took a couple of stamps and he rang to give me the price." Walter looked at me over his onion. "One was quite valuable, though not like the other one. He said it was worth maybe $125.00 and he would sell it for ninety-five. The other was worth considerably less. So I think you should look after them and store them well."

I nodded distractedly. Walter's gaze lingered a moment.

"Seems reasonable to concentrate your activity on the Commonwealth, he thought."

I looked up at Walter.

"I s'pose."

He tried again: "Did you find any others in that bag Grandad left you?"

"Yes, quite a few. I'm not sure of their value yet."

"Mr. Carruthers would know. Why don't you bring them down now that you've sorted them and he can have a look?" In fact, I had brought the Crown Royal bag with its velvety feel and gold drawstring when I first revealed the Penny Black to Mr. Carruthers, but we had both been so distracted by the finding of the rare stamp that I had not shown him any of the others collected by my great-grandfather.

"Mmm." Actually, it was a good idea. At least it gave me an excuse to go back to the town centre. All I needed now was a strategy to get Mr.

Carruthers to divulge a little more about the metal box without attracting attention or suspicion.

I removed the scowl from my face. The angry brows of a scowl, like the pouting lips of a child, I had decided, only remain efficacious for short periods of time. One had to deploy them strategically and then know when to retreat to a more pleasant demeanour. I stood and walked up to my mother. She looked me in the eyes and traced her right hand ever so gently over my left cheek. It was comforting, a gesture from my childhood. Which, in fact, I reminded myself, I was still living. I went to set the table with a lighter care.

The next day at school Mrs. Phillips was jolly, almost vivacious, which did not suit her at all. It seemed unnatural, and left us with an unaccountable impression of a leer rather than a smile. Still, it made her somewhat indulgent, from which we found little ways to profit throughout the day. Tom more than others, of course. Leese remained, as always, rather unmoved by the vagrant humours of those around her. An island of self-possession. It left one wondering what she would be like when, finally, she grew up. Cool perhaps, but not cold. Tom, on the other hand, would always be playful. Perspicacious in his own way, knowing just how far to stretch the patience of others without snapping.

The cool mornings were now decidedly frosty, almost cold. Snow would arrive soon. An anemic sun failed any longer to warm the afternoons and we had to don our coats to play outside. The light was dull and shadowless, showing up pale faces tinged with red noses. We blew short clouds of condensation as we talked and puffed around the school yard.

Mr. Maugher's room was dank now that windows could not be opened to let in fresh air. The smells of tiny reptiles and furry creatures cross-pollinated with the algae in the aquarium and the earthy tones of experimental seedlings. Tom breathed deeply from this greenhouse environment. In science class, away from the unaccustomed bubbly humour of Mrs. Phillips, I mentioned in an offhand sort of way to Tom and Leese that I would be going down to Mr. Carruthers' store after school. I did not invite them, exactly, but we did not need such niceties to be understood. Both enthusiastically said they would join me. So we went.

The brass bell tinkled discreetly from its faded red ribbon as I opened the door, slowly this time as a reluctance had overtaken me between the bus stop and the shop door. I did not speak to Tom or Leese, preferring to keep my thoughts and anxieties to myself, wondering again how I might elicit information from the reticent Mr. Carruthers, information that would help unravel the intrigue and yet not give away the knowledge that the forgery had been *intended* for my discovery. The dust motes danced in the dimming sunlight filtering through the window as the sun hung low on the horizon of a winter's early evening. The customer area, small and intimate, was dimly lit and warmly heated, dry and yet faintly musty. Mr. Carruthers had tucked himself away in the back rooms that no one ever saw, and where he undertook the serious research that he imparted sparingly to his clientele.

Leese was looking intently at the books on the shelves, but they were of little interest. The important books were not on the shelves, I guessed. They were hidden away with Mr. Carruthers. Those disposed for public perusal were stock issue and designed for the amateur. Even Leese, naturally curious, quickly reached a limitation with these. Tom was examining some specimens under the small glass case.

"See these," he pointed to a multiple printing, "they have straight edges. I thought stamps always had ragged edges."

No, I informed him, that was one of the distinguishing marks. Some of the more ancient stamps were not perforated, and the postman who had sold them would have had to cut them with a pair of scissors as he sold them. In fact, the unevenness of the cut, which made the printed image of the stamp not necessarily centred on the cut, was one of the indications of authenticity. For example, mine had no perforations, yet the wide margin on the one side indicated that it was cut from the last row of stamps printed on the larger sheet. The post man had not trimmed the stamp before selling it.

"That's correct," said Mr. Carruthers, appearing as we stared into the glass case. "Perforations were not standard in the past. Today we are starting to see self-adhesive stamps — you don't have to lick them to stick them." It was a peculiarly un-Carruthers phrase, and he seemed to smile very slightly with a playful self-satisfaction. "These self-adhesive stamps have no perforations. In the past, perforations were used simply to allow the stamps to be easily torn from the printed sheet without damaging the stamp itself. But the perforations allowed for a more exact centring of the image in a white border." He took out a sample from the display case and showed Tom how the white margins of the perforated stamp were quite even. "But the printing presses at the time were not always exact." And taking another sample, he indicated perforations that were misprinted so that the stamp appeared uncentred in the thin border. "Such a printing error is what gives this stamp its particular interest, and is the reason for its value, in fact."

Leese picked up on the point, as she would. "So it is the *im*perfection, not the perfection, which makes a stamp valuable?"

"Yes. At least sometimes."

This seemed to cause a particular delight to Leese, schooled as she was in seeking out the oddities in human processes rather than the regularities.

This was by now old news to me. And the preoccupations of the other three allowed me to cast my glance around the store without being observed. The silver box was gone.

"Thank you for the stamps you gave me last time. My father said he would pay for them." I brought out the Crown Royal whiskey bag, its felt soft from age, the golden strings drawn tightly. It was the excuse for my visit, but not the reason. I offered it to Mr. Carruthers, asking if he might go through the stamps in it as he had done with the metal box of stamps the other day.

Mr. Carruthers murmured his consent.

"Were there any other interesting stamps in that box?" I tried to sound uninterested, which was a bit silly as I was still asking the question. "You said you had not yet gone through all the stamps that were in it."

"That's correct. I have gone through everything now, but only in a cursory fashion. There are indeed some interesting stamps there. Nothing particularly rare, perhaps, but it is a collection that was put together with a good deal of thought. The person who assembled it had more than a basic knowledge of philately. There was order and deliberation in what was chosen. An amateur of some considerable knowledge and skill, I would say."

I picked up one of the stamps that Mr. Carruthers had brought out to show Tom, and I turned it over. Something struck me then. A question that now could be asked without causing suspicion because we were discussing general differences in issue, rather than the particularities of any one stamp.

I rubbed my finger over the back surface. "I think you told me once that they used to put gum on the back."

"That's a pertinent point, Ivan." Mr. Carruthers was looking straight at me and not at the stamp in my fingers. "The fact is that stamps had an adhesive and, just as we have had to do until the recent invention of the self-adhesive stamp, all a person had to do was wet the gum for the adhesive to become active and cause the stamp to stick to the envelope. It was an invention of that time which allowed stamps to be sold with the adhesive."

At this moment, the bell on the shop door tinkled and a mauve-gloved hand held the door handle as it pushed its way into the shop.

Mrs. Phillips froze when she saw me, but only for a moment, a fraction of a second with her mouth starting to open. Then she quickly blinked her eyes and the glacial, whitened cheeks flushed again with colour. Mr. Carruthers caught the suspended moment and interrupted the tension.

"Ah! Mrs. Phillips. We were just discussing your collection. I have had a chance to go through it. Well, I would call it more of an assemblage than a collection, really. Put together with some skill and not a little knowledge. Someone had tenacity and interest, if not the financial means to play the thorough-going philatelist. Still, it holds its own as an amateur collection."

Mrs. Phillips was silent, I would say hesitant, for a moment. Mr. Carruthers continued amiably, "When you first called me to the school to look through it, I was a little astonished, I admit. I wasn't expecting to find the general quality that it displayed. Someone has made discerning choices."

I remembered seeing Mr. Carruthers walking from the school with his briefcase. So that explained it. He had been out on a fact-finding mission at the request of my teacher.

"It was good of you to come," she replied rather icily. The chill on her cheek returned for a moment. She glanced almost imperceptibly in my direction. "When we had the business of Ivan here and his stamp, it got me thinking about my own collection — assemblage — that has been stored for some time. It was begun by my eldest brother, who passed away when he was still quite young. I was given it by my parents as a memento.

Eventually I took it up myself, almost as an *hommage* to my dear brother." Her words were warm, but her expression was cold.

"*Hommage.* Yes, well, I see. I understand. But did you take it up in earnest yourself, then?"

"Yes, although not at first. It took a while." A faint lifting at the edges of her lips. "It brought back some pained memories. Well, fond memories, but bitter, if you understand."

"Entirely," I heard myself say. All heads turned in my direction. Whatever prompted me to contribute, I do not know to this day. There was a tension underlying the whole exchange that demanded it. Leese looked slightly bemused, Tom was bewildered. I avoided all glances directly and looked at Mrs. Phillips. She looked blankly at me, unsure which expression to adopt. "My great-grandfather left me his collection," I ventured, "and I think about him all the time when I am working on my own."

Mr. Carruthers nodded ever so slightly.

"I wonder what he would have thought about me losing his Penny Black, his stamp. He had kept it safe for so long."

"And it is safe again, surely," Mrs. Phillips added, a fraction of a second too quickly to appear totally natural, at least to me. Perhaps the others didn't pick up on it, and maybe I was reading too much into the exchange.

Leese answered before I could formulate my thoughts, "Absolutely. It's locked away in a safety deposit box. My father has one, too, and I've gone with him to look inside."

The tension was diffused, thanks to Leese. Now I could go on without suspicion of being suspicious myself. I needed to control the conversation in order to dissemble my intentions. I was growing more proficient in verbal subterfuge.

"Did your brother have anything interesting in his collection?" I ventured in as innocent a tone as I could manage without sounding supercilious.

"Well, I'm not entirely sure. There were one or two that I thought might be of some value, although, not, of course, as valuable as yours. That's why I brought them here to Mr. Carruthers, to confirm my research."

"And I did find a few things of note," added Mr. Carruthers. "In fact, I sold two of them to Ivan just a few days ago. As you instructed, Mrs. Phillips." She smiled at him.

"Now you are well on your way, aren't you, Ivan?"

"Certainly."

Her eyes blinked. I smiled, showing just a bit of teeth.

She turned back to Mr. Carruthers. "Well, this is all happy news, then. Was there anything else?"

There was a short exchange between the two adults about stamps that Mr. Carruthers was prepared to buy and their current market value, as well as the value of her "assemblage" in general. Leese looked at me with amusement. I lifted my eyebrows and opened my eyes wide and then turned to look at the books that inhabited the sparse shelves in the small vestibule that formed the public area of the shop. I was already thoroughly familiar with the thin but judiciously displayed tools of the serious amateur collector, but I needed time to let Mrs. Phillips be diverted from any thoughts she might have about me and my growing collection. Tom glanced around the room and fingered a volume here and there. He wiped a shelf with his index finger and looked at the dust on his fingertip. It seemed an incongruous gesture for one who never paid attention to the scattered and eclectic shrapnel lodged in his room.

The voices ended abruptly; the transaction had been sorted out and concluded with the finality of silence. Mrs. Phillips was donning her mauve gloves and looking a little petulant. Mr. Carruthers arranged some papers in a heavy drawer below the glass display case. He slid the drawer shut and locked it with a black and ancient key.

Mrs. Phillips nodded in our general direction and left the shop, the door clanging noisily as the bell rang shrill in the cold evening air. Despite the blast of almost-winter air that filled the shop, the room seemed somehow warmer.

CHAPTER TWELVE

D uring the ride home Leese sat silently, ruminating. She glanced at me occasionally and then turned quickly away. Once or twice she seemed on the verge of opening her mouth to say something, and then she stopped her tongue and bit her lip. Oblivious, Tom chattered away about how odd it was to see Mrs. Phillips in the shop. Teachers, apparently, only lived in classrooms, like caged beasts in a zoo, having no personality, no wants or needs or interests apart from what the student wanted, needed, or sought. But then again, I had visited her house. Well, the alleyway behind her house. And I knew that something else breathed outside that well-lit classroom. Shadows take no hold in a classroom of learning, as if truth admits neither shade nor obscurity outside the stream of its luminosity. And yet valuable and treasured things can go missing as easily in the broad reaches of light as in the cold lengths of shade.

Finally, Leese interrupted Tom midway through some observation on the early dawn of twilight and the astronomical mechanics of the approaching winter solstice. Interesting as it was, neither Leese nor I was paying much attention. Tom politely demurred as Leese broke in. His was not a domineering nature, and he did not expect others to enter into the joy of his own musings. Leese, on the other hand, had rather less sympathy for those whose interests were peripheral to her own.

"Yes, but…" she began without any intention to take up Tom's theme. "Yes, but why would Mrs. Phillips take her stamp collection in for valuation now?"

"Well, she just learned Ivan found something really valuable," offered Tom, abandoning the winter solstice for speculations on human behaviour. This was not his forte.

"Maybe she knew it might be valuable; after all, her brother had left it to her and she must have known something about it."

"Well," I offered, "what a stamp is worth changes all the time. Maybe she just wanted a more recent appraisal."

"And Ivan's Penny Black made her interested again," Tom ventured. Cause and effect were his domain, although in the more impersonal realm of natural science than that of human conduct.

"Certainly," Leese concluded. Mr. Carruthers' idiom was being picked up by all of us. It was changing the mode of our conversation as Mrs. Phillips was altering the object. "And yet she is so organized and so… methodical." The word pleased her. "It just doesn't seem like her to have something she doesn't know all about."

This type of conjecture was beyond Tom. "Hmmm."

"Can either of you remember anything in particular about the day I brought the Penny Black to school?" I was wondering what I had overlooked. I had been distracted when it went missing, and yet all the other students were gathered around it.

"What do you mean?" asked Tom, blinking.

I was going nowhere in my own speculations. I needed fresh eyes to look at the whole scenario.

"I mean, isn't it peculiar, Tom, that the stamp could go missing right under everyone's eyes? Mr. Carruthers had put it in his briefcase to take it to the bank with my dad and me. How did it disappear from his briefcase? He's very careful about things, too."

"Was it in his briefcase then?" Leese asked. None of us seemed to recall. "We were all looking at my stretched sheepskin," she added, referring to the last will and testament she had brought to show and tell.

"And my paper," Tom added.

"Well, your wet mess that you were trying to turn into paper…"

"Whatever… Sheepskin. Parchment. Paper."

"We weren't looking at the stamp at all," I realized. Everyone had already gone up to look at the Penny Black when Mr. Carruthers went to inspect Leese's cherished document. "What was everyone else doing?"

Silence.

"Everyone had gone back to the things that they had brought for show and tell," Leese said slowly, not so much remembering as drawing an inference from probable human behaviour. "We were packing up and getting ready to go home."

"Mr. Carruthers had put the Penny Black in my stamp catalogue and left it on the table. Then he went to see you, Leese. So that was the only time it was left unwatched. It couldn't have been for more than a few minutes."

"So someone must have taken the stamp out of the catalogue quickly while Mr. Carruthers was with both of you and after we had all finished looking at it," I concluded. "No way anyone in our class could do it."

"There was only one person who wasn't packing up with us," Leese said, drawing out her inference. We looked at one another.

"Teachers don't steal," Tom said. Then added, "And how would she be able to produce a forgery so quickly?"

We discussed the forgery. "All you need is to find an old scrap of paper like the one the Penny Black is printed on, something that looks authentic enough," Tom said.

"It was easy enough for me to find old paper, like the old wills you can still find sometimes," Leese reflected. "And you just need a tiny blank square where you could copy the image of the stamp. My documents have lots of blank space around the writing."

"So whoever took the stamp had enough time to look around," Tom said. "The old techniques I was trying to use were very common back then. It was pretty common stock… pretty common sort of paper," he said. "It wouldn't take much looking."

"Easy enough" — proof of my conclusion.

I told Tom and Leese about my observations of Mr. Carruthers leaving the school and of my visit to the lane behind Mrs. Phillips' house. I gave them my conclusions, too. I surmised that Mr. Carruthers had been asked by Mrs. Phillips to come to the school to look at her collection. I thought maybe, somehow, they had colluded, but that now seemed impossible. How could they have arranged everything in the short time that we were all together in the classroom? It was too elaborate. Something simpler had to have happened.

It was relatively easy to make a duplicate of the image of the stamp good enough to fool and buy time, but reproducing the time-worn adhesive on the back was omitted. It was an easy oversight, but one which I was now sure was the proof of my conclusion. I explained it to Tom and Leese.

"Are you sure?" Tom asked.

"That's why I was asking Mr. Carruthers about the gum — the glue — on the back of stamps just now. It was the evidence I needed to confirm it."

"And he did," said Leese with finality. I nodded.

There was silence as the bus jostled us over bumps and around corners.

"So now what?" Tom's voice was barely audible.

"So now what?" Leese repeated.

"If she really took it, where would she keep it? At first I think she hid it in our attendance folder on her desk." And I explained how it had disappeared and moved around in the days after the stamp was lost and before the forgery was discovered.

"Right under our noses," said Leese with a sneer. "Right in front of everyone."

"Sometimes the things right in front of us are the things we never see," said Tom. "Mrs. Phillips just kept on with what she always did. And no one ever thought…"

"Perhaps," I said, "but she was acting strange for a few days, don't you remember? What was she up to then?"

"I wonder," Leese began, and then broke off. We looked at her while she turned something over in her mind. "Would she keep the Penny Black where she had kept the other stamps before? In her garden shed?"

And so a plan was formed at last, though not a very clever or elaborate one. We would all go to her lane and try to get into her shed. If the plan was simple, it still needed some thinking through. When would she be away from home? How to get into a locked shed? And, I now knew from experience, it had to be done before the snow stayed on the ground for winter. I didn't want any footprints left behind.

It would be another six days before the morning sprinklings of snow thawed. In the meantime, we had set ourselves up to track the daily movements of Mrs. Phillips. Her regularity and obsessive order betrayed her to us. A creature of habit follows a map of daily life. Since there were three of us, we could tag-team plotting her behavioural cartography, making it appear as if we just happened to be around by chance, and then trading off so that if she noticed our presence, it would appear a random presence first of one, then of the other. It is not as easy as one might think to appear to be doing one thing aimlessly while in fact engaging deliberately to accomplish another. Even at eleven years old when purposeful activity is frequently lacking, feigning carelessness requires a certain art and planning. There is a delicate distinction between appearing shiftless and appearing shifty, and one not easy to achieve. The former might arouse, at most, annoyance, but the latter could arouse suspicion. And while it is good to avoid both annoyance and suspicion when engaged in covert observation, it is always preferable to risk the first but ever to avoid the second.

Mrs. Phillips set out from her home precisely at 8:12 every morning. Living so close to the school, she arrived by 8:26, always carrying a large purse that contained a thermos of coffee or tea and a lunch. She never seemed to carry anything else. No papers, no teaching plan, no tests to mark. These were all done before she left the school at the end of the day, and everything was locked away in her desk with her lesson plan in the left middle drawer, and her marking papers in the bottom. The attendance folder, as we knew, was never locked away.

Because she finished her teaching tasks before she left the school, her time of departure varied according to the day's activities, but generally she perused her lesson plan for the next day just before she shut up her desk. She never left later than 4:50 and never earlier than 3:45. There was something reassuring in such regularity.

Her evenings were spent on various diversions. On Tuesday she was met by someone who looked like it might be her mother. Mrs. Phillips stepped out from her front door at precisely 5:00 as the putative mother drove up. They drove away together, presumably for dinner. Mondays were spent at home. The light in the kitchen and living room remained on. We didn't get a chance to see what she did on a Sunday as we all stayed at home with our own families. But on Saturday we decided to check on her home individually at 10:00 a.m., 2:00 p.m., and 5:00 p.m., dividing up the times so that our own parents would be less suspicious of our outings. Friday was also an "at home" evening, but this time friends stopped by for dinner. Wednesday we did not follow up, but Thursday, the first evening we scoped out her home after getting off the bus, we noticed that she was gone by 6:00, the hour when we had arrived. She was back by 9:00 p.m. because I surreptitiously escaped Walter and Macy to take a quick look at her home at that hour. It was curious that there was no Mr. Phillips. Was he dead? Or, I suddenly thought, maybe he had been knocked off. But then, with a shudder, I dismissed the idea as pure speculation.

Walter and Macy did not make much inquiry as to my frequent absences during these six days. I offered vague intimations of visiting Leese or Tom or both, which was true at least in the large sense. We were alternating our visits at various times, and so meeting at least in intention if not in fact. I knew that Walter and Macy questioned the explanations for my absences, but, as always, they gave me a great deal of leeway and the benefit of any doubts they might have formulated.

We drew up a weekday calendar of our teacher's activities, assuming that she would be as punctual and regular in her occupations after school as she was during school hours. The scope for our investigations was limited, but we were worried about an early onset of winter and snow. We needed to strike quickly before the opportunity was lost entirely. We had adequate but imperfect knowledge. It would have to be sufficient.

We decided that a Tuesday would be best, and we hoped that meeting her mother for supper at 5:00 p.m. was a weekly tradition. It was an awkward time for us as our suppers were also being prepared at that time, but we managed to convince our respective parents that we would be staying after school for a little while to complete a project. Then we could just say we had lost track of the time. It was evasive, but not false. Tuesday morning was one of those silent winter mornings, with a grey sky and a pale sun that struggled to beat down a waxen moon and vie for victory in the heavens. A light snowfall of thin, dry flakes was swept aside rather than shovelled. It took only a weak breath of wind to clear the path. But a morning such as this gives little away as to what will come. Either the sun will succeed and burn away the wisps of cloud, or a heavy snow will win the day and begin winter in earnest. We could only carry out our plan if there was no snow on the ground by evening, and no trace of footsteps in Mrs. Phillips' garden. My footprints were big, those of an adult, but the footprints of Leese and Tom would still betray the work of elder children.

I wasn't sure how I would enter the shed. I remembered that it had a padlock. Would she lock it? Probably. She was not a negligent person or one given to forgetfulness. If I couldn't get in, then we would have to call it off and think of another plan. But I knew that there was no other plan. My one glimmer of hope was the thought that she would not want to be caught with the stamp, and so would avoid the more obvious and legitimate places to hide it. A safety deposit box would have to be rented in her own name. Keeping it in her house would incriminate her too. For some peculiar reason she had kept her brother's stamp collection in the little garden shed. This was so out of character that it almost made sense. Perhaps she used the shed as storage for things which were of little importance to her, and learning the surprising value of the Penny Black sparked a hope of windfall profit for herself where before only a sentimental value was acknowledged. Mrs. Phillips did not seem the sentimental sort, and so a back-garden shed might be the appropriate place to house such valueless items. But where did she keep the things she valued? Or hide a treasure that did not belong to her?

Here was the biggest problem, it occurred to me, and I talked it over with Leese and Tom after school as we waited for Mrs. Phillips to glance through her lesson plan and end her working day. "If the Penny Black is something no one has seen before, then it's unique, right?"

"Right," said Leese.

"So if she *does* try to sell it, all the experts would know it is unique and they would be excited by the new discovery."

"Right."

"So she can't sell it. She's stuck."

Leese was turning this over. "If she tries to sell it at a stamp fair or something, she would draw attention to herself and everyone would want to know where she got it from."

"That would mean she would have to say what had happened in the classroom," Tom continued with the thought, "and she can't want that because it would look suspicious." Here he stopped for a moment. "But she wants the money, doesn't she? She just doesn't want everyone to know that she's trying to sell it."

"'Cause the stamp is supposed to be in your dad's safety deposit box." Leese was working something out in her head. Mrs. Phillips could hardly want to revisit the events of the theft and risk revealing herself. Tom and I were quiet. This was Leese's domain, plumbing the machinations of human deception.

So what does one do with a unique and publicly recognizable asset? Where do thieves hide a stolen painting? To whom do they sell it? Who would buy it?

Leese had the answer. "She would sell it to a collector who loves to collect but isn't interested in the money. Someone who wants to hoard it for his own personal satisfaction because he really likes owning something unique. He's happy just knowing that it's unique and valuable and he isn't interested in selling it again to get the money." She worked out the details. "The person would sell it to someone who isn't afraid of the risk, or rather, someone who knows how to reduce the risk because he isn't interested in reselling it for money. His interest is in *possession*.

"I read about people who have their own art galleries just for themselves. They never let anyone see what they have. They have a collection just for themselves to see."

Tom broke in, "I'd like to have my own private collection of planets!" which was ridiculous. Leese pursed her lips in contempt of such idle fancies. "I would." Tom stifled a laugh that came out as a sort of whimper.

I laughed with him, without making a sound, as Leese applied her thoughts to less childish plots. "There must be people who have private stamp collections that they never tell anyone about."

An unspoken question between us hung in the air: So, how does one find out who this faceless person is who gathers but who does not wish to reap?

Tom hesitated, taking in this information which he had never before thought about. After a moment, his eyes opened wide like he had just discovered a new natural species or a star. "Actually," he began a little formally, quite satisfied with himself, "the crucial moment for the hoarder — the moment when he is most at risk of being discovered — is not the moment when he *possesses* the stamp he is after, but the moment when he has to reveal himself as the *buyer*." And he crossed his arms in triumph, looking quite smug. Mr. Carruthers would have approved. Leese certainly did. Tom had come down from the planets at last.

"So," Leese picked up the thread, "the real buyer must hide behind someone else." In other words, there must be a mediator who assumes the risk of discovery, but in such a way that even if discovered, he still conceals the true purchaser's identity. Leese was in her element, wondering about the complexities of subterfuge that mask the real person. "The buyer would have to be someone with a lot of money to buy the stamp, but also someone who could convince someone else to act for themselves in a way that couldn't be traced." Discretion and concealment were the key elements at the moment of greatest risk, the moment of acquiring the unique thing of value.

As we talked through the matter, it became clear to us that not only the buyer of a stolen masterpiece needed to insist on absolute discretion and concealment, but the seller too. Paintings on the public market were sold by reputable owners, even if sold to anonymous buyers. But stolen paintings were not sold by reputable owners, indeed not by the owners at all, but by the thieves or accomplices, who themselves disguised the identity of the thief.

We entered the back laneway at 4:55 p.m., after listening for the approaching car of Mrs. Phillips' mother. It came precisely at 5:00 as anticipated. Tom doubled over, anchoring his hands on his knees and squatting so that I could plant my two feet on his shoulders and pull myself more easily over the top of the fence. He grunted loudly as I stepped onto the rungs of this makeshift ladder while Leese glanced furtively around, enjoying herself immensely. In a second, I had scampered over the fence and landed squarely in the back garden on a stone path. The snow had melted during the day and left a light dampness over the ground. I could just barely discern the squinted eyes of Leese and Tom through the narrow interstices of the fence boards. If I hadn't been so nervous, I would have laughed. I glanced around the yard, meticulously prepared for the inhospitable winter months, perfect furrows tilled and waiting for spring. I looked into the windows of the house but they were dark and blank. It was dark outside too, and I would be hard to see from inside the house. I crouched near the door of the shed, although crouching served no purpose. I suppose when one is skulking over trespassed lands, one naturally wants to appear as small as possible, even Ivan the Giant. I doubted that Captain America would have skulked, but then again, his was the world of comic books and obvious villains. I was mired in the reality of suburban thieves masked as ordinary neighbours.

Leese and Tom whispered indiscernible things through the boards. I was afraid to answer in the silence of the back garden. I pulled at the padlock but it was locked against intruders. I went back to the fence. It was Leese, again, who read the mind of our teacher. "I think she might keep a key hidden nearby."

There was not much nearby. In summer there might have been a potted plant or a stray trellis, but winter provided few sheltered places to hide a key. Nevertheless, I looked about. Nothing on the door frame itself, as I slid a finger along the top. The shed was close up against the fence boards. I felt along the side of the shed hidden by its proximity to the fence and was rewarded when I felt cold metal wedged between lengths of horizontal wooden siding. I pried the key from its hiding place and held it up for Leese and Tom to see, then unlocked the door to the shed.

Inside it was dark. I had brought a small flashlight and I used it to survey the contents. If this was the place where Mrs. Phillips stored her sentimental trove, she was hard-hearted indeed. There was not much in it. There were a few shelves of storage boxes filled with childhood toys made of wood. Each box had a label describing the contents in the terse, even script which I recognized from the classroom chalkboard: "trains" and "dolls" and, what I thought was peculiar, "ducks." Were they toys from her own childhood? For some reason, I couldn't imagine Mrs. Phillips having children of her own to give the toys to. Children would have wreaked havoc upon her ordered routine. But then again, she had dedicated her life to teach children, so who was to say? Who could plumb the heart of her motives?

On a little shelf, high up and close to the open rafters, my narrow stream of light flashed off a metal canister. It was the box where she had kept the stamps. It would have been a stretch for her to put it up there. I inspected it to make sure it was the same one. It was. I put the flashlight down and opened the lid. I felt inside, and then picked up the light to see inside. It was empty. Even her brother's worthless stamps were gone.

CHAPTER THIRTEEN

I knew it was unlikely that Mrs. Phillips would have stored her purloined treasure in the garden shed. It was interesting, however, that she had restored the empty tin to its place, devoid even of her brother's less valuable collection. I wasn't downhearted by the lack of discovery. Collectively, Leese, Tom, and I had exercised a small degree of surveillance successfully and, as far as we were aware, we had been undetected. There was a certain amount of thrill just in that. Tom seemed particularly invigorated by the task of observation. I suppose that fit in with his penchant to study reptiles and assorted smelly vermin. Leese was proving adept at discerning human motives, which helped to point us in the direction where we should look. I wasn't sure yet where my skills lay. Patterns were what I looked for, mathematical precision, not the indiscernible motives of human choice or the discovery of irregularity in observable data.

Mrs. Phillips had departed from her pattern of behaviour. Or had she? I couldn't tell. She had been predictability itself and now she had launched herself into the unpredictable. She had shown no interest in stamps when I declared my intention to take up philately as a hobby. Now she was visiting Mr. Carruthers with a collection of stamps, said to be her brother's. The collection, it is true, had nothing like the Penny Black, but what amateur stamp collection does? There were, in fact, some notable stamps among those picked by her brother, which would indicate that he had some knowledge behind the choices he had made — if it really was the brother who had made them. I would never know because I had no way to confirm the truth about a deceased relative of my teacher.

"You know," I said after we had left the alley and were slowly walking back, "I don't think Mrs. Phillips would have any interest in holding on to a valuable stamp. When she found out the value of my Penny Black, she took her whole collection to Mr. Carruthers so he could appraise it. That's not the pattern of someone obsessed with *possessing* something valuable."

Leese agreed. "She probably just wants to get rid of your stamp. She just wants the money. After all, if she keeps your stamp and then someone finds it, she might be charged with theft."

"She probably wants to get rid of it as soon as possible," Tom said.

"Well, she just doesn't seem like someone who would take such a big risk. She's too... ordered, and... methodical." Leese was searching for the words. "She thinks things out before she does anything."

"Except this time," I pointed out. "How does someone like her who is so careful just suddenly shift gears and steal something right in front of her, in front of a whole classroom of people?"

"A classroom of *children*," Leese pointed out.

"And two adults," Tom said. "It was still pretty risky. Like you said, Leese, she doesn't like to take risks."

"Maybe that's the thing, though," I said slowly. "Maybe she didn't even think of the risk. Maybe she just did it. She *could* do it because she didn't plan it at all. She just didn't think."

"That sounds like us, not her," Tom said.

"Well, maybe you and Ivan," Leese corrected.

Leese had a point. I had rarely thought things through before I acted, so, in a way, I could see this. Act as the opportunity presents itself or as need dictates, and then think the consequences through afterwards, or suffer them passively if no other option opens up. Mrs. Phillips would now be thinking through the consequences and trying desperately to open up her options. For a couple of days after the stamp went missing, she had been distracted and had let her routine fall away. But since then, her default pattern had reasserted itself with greater discipline, and the forgery mysteriously appeared. She was back in her comfort zone. She must have calculated a way around the risk of being caught in the short term and was working on a way to get rid of the Penny Black and profit in the long term. This gave a window of opportunity, but for how long no one could know.

Mr. Carruthers was the type of philatelist who enjoyed possessing a valuable and famous stamp. Hadn't he mentioned that he had some valuable ones in his own possession? He also knew the worth of things and knew how to sell and buy. Perhaps he would know how a thief quietly and anonymously sells a stolen stamp.

After talking this through we decided on a two-pronged plan of action. We would see where it led and then decide. First, we would continue to watch Mrs. Phillips to observe whether her weekly pattern confirmed itself over the longer term. And secondly, we would pay a visit to Mr. Carruthers to uncover how stolen stamps are resold outside of the public market.

Mr. Carruthers smiled when we walked into the shop. We were a novelty to his regular order and even Mr. Carruthers, it seemed, could appreciate novelty. Whereas Mrs. Phillips smiled only when she had to, which gave her smiling countenance a rather threatening look, Mr. Carruthers' smile bid welcome. It promised respite from his toiling in a way that he found pleasing, and he magnanimously beamed his enjoyment to all of us. Tom responded well to this unspoken overture and began chatting him up with a summary of our day and the demands by Mrs. Phillips that filled our daylight hours. He was surprisingly detailed about our teacher's habits in the classroom and the almost unvarying metronome of classroom activity. I could almost see Mrs. Phillips tapping out the minutes and cycles of subjects and pauses. Math-2-3, Spelling-5-6, Reading-8-9. Our rhythmic cycle of daily life. While I had always found some satisfaction in the ordered beat of the day, I think I began to understand Tom's desire to crush the clock with random acts of rebellion, his sort of evolutionary cry thrust into the void of monotony. Mr. Carruthers bent over his ancient glass display case with patient amusement.

"And you say Mrs. Phillips is always so structured in her daily management of your scholastic employment?" he prodded with a little shine radiating from his eyes, a glint that even pierced the thick eyeglass lenses that usually obscured any clear gaze. It was hard to read him sometimes because the distorted lenses blocked any attempt to read his thoughts through his pupils. Eyes are the windows of the soul, it is said.

"Yes," Tom affirmed. Then he added quite superfluously, "Invariably." A very slight movement at the corners of Mr. Carruthers' mouth caused Tom to smile. In that dusty, uncluttered, but full little shopfront, we were all lifted up in a way that seemed natural and which spurned the condescension children are so used to. One could be frank with Mr. Carruthers. Polite and tactful, but direct.

"And so she sees to your advancement."

"Yes." Tom hesitated for a fraction of a second. "Well, to our *scholastic* advancement."

"I see. And you have other types of advancement to which she is not committed."

Tom hesitated again. "Yes."

"Like stamp collecting," I added quickly, trying to find a way to raise the matter we had all come down here for. "I didn't know that she was interested in stamps until I saw her here, in your shop, yesterday."

"Nor did I." It was the answer I had been looking for. "She did not mention it that day at school when the stamp disappeared, and I had never seen her here before. She telephoned shortly after and I met her at the school to discuss the legacy left her by her bother."

"I suppose people don't really think about stamps as having much value."

"Perhaps not. But even for serious stamp collectors the value is rarely in the prices they might get for their collection. Oh, of course we all hope to discover that one rare exception, such as yours, Ivan. And very lucky too. But most of us gain little satisfaction from that. It's something else — a little hard to explain — that draws us in and keeps us coming back."

"I think I'm starting to understand that," I added. Mr. Carruthers blinked at me in that odd way he had that said everything and precisely nothing at the same time. It was dark outside now. The early wintry evenings had lost their sun and somehow in the dimly lit room the atmosphere was now more intimate. Humans huddled against the elements and the unseen, unlit faces outside. "It's the possession, not the…"

"…dispossession. The acquiring and not the surrender," Mr. Carruthers finished my thought. "To forfeit possession for pure monetary profit is not the motive that keeps collectors collecting."

"Otherwise you would have nothing," Leese interrupted. Mr. Carruthers nodded at her.

"Precisely."

"But what if someone finds out they have something valuable and isn't interested in collecting it, but in…" Leese was looking again for just the right word, "forfeiting it?"

"That is a part of my purpose. I match up buyers and sellers."

"And what would happen if, perhaps… well, let's say someone has a stamp that they shouldn't have, that they've stolen. They don't want it as their possession; they want to sell it and take the money. We were talking about that amongst ourselves. It's like someone who steals a famous painting. How do they sell it without getting caught?"

Mr. Carruthers did not answer right away. He waited a moment. A long moment, it felt to me. I was glad Leese had asked the question rather than me. If it had come from me, I feared that he would suspect I was fishing for something. Which I definitely was.

"That's a difficult question. It is easier to sell a stolen painting — or stamp," he turned from Leese to look at me, "to a real collector who isn't interested in re-selling it, but rather to holding onto it. That way no one finds it again, and the buyer obtains satisfaction merely by possessing it. The seller gets his financial reward and the collector, remaining anonymous, still obtains the reward that is most important to him, to be able to examine the stamp at will, in the privacy of his own collection. There are other types of buyers, however, who are less interested in possessing the stamp. They will hold the stamp, hoping its value will go up after many years when everyone has given up hope of finding it again. Then they slip the stamp back onto the market with far less risk of detection. Sometimes they invent a story of how the stamp has suddenly come into their possession. A little like your own miraculous find, Ivan." I fidgeted uncomfortably. "Of course, you were not inventing the story of your great-grandfather." I formed a "no" with my lips, but no sounds came from my mouth. "By then it is years after the theft was reported and it is almost impossible to retrace the steps of the original thief. They can sell it at a much higher price." He glanced at all three of us in turn. "Of course, it presupposes someone of significant wealth who can afford to hold onto the stamp — or the painting — for a very long time. It is easier with stamps than with paintings."

"So, in those cases, how does the thief find a buyer?"

"That *is* the question, isn't it?" he said, simply.

He backed away from his glass case. "Come here for a moment." We followed him down a narrow hallway that was very dark. A single light bulb strained to wrest the space from total obscurity. It was a hallway much longer than it would seem possible. A few doors on the right were tightly closed and no light emitted through any possible cracks. We could hear each other breathing. Mr. Carruthers stopped for a very short moment at a door that closed off the hallway. He did not look around at us. Carefully he placed his fingers around the door handle. A short, smooth, electric scraping revealed that a heavy deadbolt was sliding away. Twisting the door handle, he led us into a void that was illuminated at first by a ring of soft light emanating from the perimeters where the wall reached to the floor. The white floor gleamed, but the light accentuated its uneven texture. It was formed from wide, ancient planks of floorboard, painted in brilliant gloss to reflect upwards. As we entered, the room slowly revealed itself. The system of lighting only gradually reached its full luminosity, and even then the room was not what one would call brightly lit, but it was all pure white, and what light there was reflected from the surfaces so that it was not harsh, but somehow soft and confiding.

The room was such a contrast to the shopfront that it disoriented me. No dusty streams of sunlight from street level windows, no unpainted wood anywhere, no shelves. Only plates of glass from intricately placed frames lining all the walls, and all the frames where white. The glass in the frames did not reflect the light but somehow seemed to absorb it and then radiate it around the room. In each frame was a tiny parcel of colour, which, as the light rose and as my eyes adjusted, revealed itself to be a stamp, a unique stamp in each frame, the frame much too large for the coloured blot but which enhanced the interest of each. Above us, a high, narrow gallery ran the perimeter and a white staircase offset at a corner of the room wound upwards. Otherwise, the space was open, but closed against any natural light. There were no windows. It was not a wide room but it was very long. The air hissed and it was clear that the air, light, temperature, and probably the humidity were all carefully controlled.

In the centre of the room were placed only three items: a round table on a curved pedestal all of white, like a jewel cast in its setting, glinting like the high gloss of the floor, and two chairs, also white and without any harsh corners, commanding the space on either side of the table.

It was so unlike anything else in that place, including Mr. Carruthers himself, that it left all three of us subdued. When finally we spoke, it was in half-tones and measured sentences.

"This is my own collection," Mr. Carruthers explained. "It is here, too, that I sometimes meet with a buyer or seller who has a particular interest. It is quite secure."

It did not seem that any response was expected of us. "If I were the possessor of your Penny Black, Ivan, it would find its way in here." He glanced up and around with equanimity. "It would be quite safe." There was no door other than the one by which we had entered.

"As safe as my father's safety deposit box," I murmured.

"Quite."

"But a little bigger," Tom murmured. Mr. Carruthers smiled ever so slightly.

"I once had a man come here who was looking to buy a stamp. He looked a very ordinary sort of man. Not one you would remark upon if you passed him on the street. But he was a man of enormous wealth and he was used to collecting things. Or more precisely, he was used to owning things, possessing things, if you will. He was rather indifferent to the things once he owned them. It was curious, but once he possessed something, he seemed to forget about it. He would be obsessed with obtaining it, by whatever means he could. But once obtained, the game, for him, was over. He cherished the thing only in an abstract way. He derived no enjoyment from gazing upon it. His pleasure was in the hunt. And when his pleasure was spent, well, then his enjoyment was a little tinged with… disappointment. If obtaining the thing was difficult, so much more was his pleasure increased. And his obsession." Here Mr. Carruthers paused and looked at me, then, uncharacteristically, he looked away. He looked upwards, as if the conundrum could be answered in the great space above.

"If he had to spend vast sums to obtain the thing then he somehow seemed more satisfied, as if the victory were greater when measured against a paper currency." Again, he stopped for a moment. "Strange. I have collected all my life, and it is true that the search for something of great worth is a motive in itself. Yet the search remains only the means and not the end. A little stamp, hardly large enough to merit a frame..." He glanced around the many frames in his white room, frames that were many sizes too large for the stamps they presented. "The stamp is the thing that drives the search. But it was not so for him. It could be a painting or a piece of furniture. Anything that others wanted, anything that was rare and unique such that no one else could have it if he alone possessed it, this was the motive behind his search. He had to *have* so that others have *not*."

Leese had become quite oblivious to the things around her, captivated by the words she heard.

"This did not make him a likeable man, although he had a charm, to be sure. A charm that he wielded with effect to accomplish his end. He had charmed a lot of things from many persons, no doubt.

"What he wanted, I did not possess. Yet he wanted it still. He wanted me to find it and to facilitate its transfer to him, regardless of the cost. He wanted it, it was clear, regardless of the method required to obtain it. I had the strange impression that the more devious the method, the more he would be satisfied." Mr. Carruthers shivered almost imperceptibly. "It is not my way," he proffered by way of conclusion to his tale. He glanced around his room again.

"And did you find what he wanted?" Leese asked.

"Yes, although only after a very painstaking and intense search. But the owner was a true collector and he would not yield."

"So what happened?"

Mr. Carruthers shrugged as he looked at nothing in particular. "The transaction was not effected."

"So the man never got his stamp."

"Of that I'm not certain. There was news of a robbery and the collection was pillaged. The unique stamp disappeared. Eventually the robbers were caught, but the stamp never reappeared and it remains missing to this day. The thieves were unable to identify the person who had hired them, and so the story ends there." We remained in silence. For a moment, Mr. Carruthers seemed to fold deep within his memory to pinpoint a remembrance that displeased him. His gaze fixed upon nothing in his private museum. "I had a thorough knowledge of my... craft. That knowledge brought me a certain renown, and a certain pride at that time. But my knowledge did not extend to the ways of men. I let slip the name of the collector and that was a grave error, a grave error in judgment. I was then too inexperienced to understand the consequences of an error in judgment. Much that was valuable in my little world was lost." And the thought of that irretrievable loss drew a pained furrow across his brow.

"But enough of that." He smiled through his pallid features. "You have nothing but what lies before you. And that is a hopeful thought."

He led us out of the cloistered room and back to the now-darkened storefront with its tangible wood and dusty light wavering under ceiling lamps. The daylight outside had completely abandoned us, and the solitary brass bell on the faded ribbon tinkled weakly, ushering us into the still early night as he shut the door and closed his shop.

CHAPTER FOURTEEN

It was peculiar, but the three of us left Mr. Carruthers' shop with a renewed sense of what needed to be done, and the immediate thing that needed doing was to trace the pattern of activity of our teacher. We quickly organized a schedule in order to confirm the results of our first watch. If Mrs. Phillips had robbed me of my inheritance, I wanted to know how she would go about disposing of it. Obviously, she could not reveal it to Mr. Carruthers. Would she seek out another person to be her middleman? Another Mr. Carruthers? It seemed unlikely, since finding another Mr. Carruthers, we were certain, would prove to be impossible. Furthermore, she had a limited time frame in which to work. She needed to sell the Penny Black quickly and anonymously. The only other solution that we could think of was that she would find someone to approach Mr. Carruthers in her place. But this too was problematical. She could hardly hide behind someone else and blatantly tell Mr. Carruthers that what was for sale was my Penny Black. He had seen it, and he assumed (as far as I knew) that it was in my possession, safely secured in a safety deposit box.

If my Penny Black were suddenly on the market, the game would be up. My dad would be contacted and then it would be proved that I had been given a fake, easily detected because hastily improvised. Mr. Carruthers would recognize the forgery within minutes, with the obvious conclusion that the one offering to sell the young Victoria was a thief, or colluding with a thief.

I drew up a grid with times of day and established a rotation by which one of us would fill each slot. We only needed to observe Mrs. Phillips' after-school habits. I filled in what we already knew. None of us could cover her supper hours without attracting some suspicion from our own families, so we had to let that go. We developed some cover stories that, while not outright lies, nevertheless stretched the boundaries of truth. Something can be both very precisely correct and yet not quite accurate. "I need to work on a school project with Leese" is very precise. Tracking the movements of our suspect was, indeed, a school project in which we all collaborated. Mrs. Phillips was, after all, our teacher. However, failing to specify that I was not actually going to Leese's home to collaborate on the project was the omission of a fact that we hoped would remain hidden. Tom's home lay a little farther than Mrs. Phillips' house, so that "I am heading over to Tom's to work on a project" was strictly correct; I just would never quite arrive at Tom's house after heading over. I didn't feel good about this sort of dissimulation, but I didn't know what else to do until I had better proof.

"We need to make sure Mrs. Phillips' activities are the same each week," I explained. "The hours when she isn't doing her routine things will give us the times when she is free to find someone to sell my stamp."

Tom and Leese agreed. Leese, of course, picked up the thread, "And the people she meets might also be the list of the suspects she would send to contact Mr. Carruthers about selling it."

Tom rarely suspected anyone of anything, so he just looked at Leese. He remained dubious. He simply could not understand any intention to deceive. It made him a trusted friend but, admittedly, a rather useless sleuth. I could put x and y together, Tom could map out the stars, but Leese alone was at home pondering the unreachable depths of human deception.

"At least," Tom hesitated, uncertain about his conclusion, "at least the person she uses wouldn't know who we are, or," he continued slowly, "or know that the stamp belongs to us — or any student of Mrs. Phillips. If they did, that would put Mrs. Phillips in a difficult spot."

Leese glowed at him with new appreciation.

"The less the person she chooses knows about the circumstances which… which allowed her to acquire the Penny Black, the better for her. Otherwise, that person might come directly to us… well… to you, Ivan, or your dad, to get a better deal. They could also blackmail Mrs. Phillips if they thought Mrs. Phillips had put herself in a difficult position by unpremeditated" — the word seemed to please Leese immensely and it kind of rolled off her lips — "unpremeditated theft."

I brought our thoughts to a comforting conclusion. "So we're safe from detection." We would be invisible to the one person who would matter. In the meantime, we had to make sure we remained invisible while we confirmed the movements of Mrs. Phillips, who would certainly recognize us if she saw us outside her home.

The early evenings provided natural cover and winter hats and hoods obscured our facial features under any streetlamp. We were able to fill out some of the details of her life, which by and large observed a steady routine. Nothing surprising there. We could only manage two and a half weeks of observation before our parents started to subtly question the motives for our actions, so to break off suspicion we had to suspend our surveillance. Nevertheless, we had gained some satisfaction that our short inventory of Mrs. Phillips' life in its larger context reflected a steady and regular cycle of events. But, like all such routines, it was a cycle dictated by her own interests and choices. Mondays were "at home" evenings. Tuesdays remained consecrated to an outing with her mother, presumably supper. Wednesdays, which we had not previously observed, revealed a new dimension to her personality that we had nowhere witnessed before, because on Wednesdays she escaped her home with a violin case in hand. I had once heard that the violin was the instrument most resembling the human voice. I don't know if that is true, but it was intriguing to think that she had need of another voice, but one whose pitch and variations mimicked her own. Where she went with it, we never discovered. Lessons? An amateur chamber music trio? At least it gave colour to her life which, in so much else, resembled a winterscape of greys and blues. Thursdays she was absent again, but always leaving precisely at 5:00 p.m. to return at 8:00 p.m. She left her home with nothing in her grasp and returned as empty-handed as she had left. Since, outside of the classroom, the dynamics of her life remained to us an enigma, it was difficult to imagine how she filled these three hours a week. Even in her approach to teaching, she left nothing slip that ever revealed a personal note or a ledger of private reckoning. Her teaching was closed off to the intimate sphere of living. It was efficient, but dead, and her lifeless day made it difficult to speculate on an evening's resurrection. Fridays were reserved for a circle of friends. Evidently a small circle, for the same people reappeared in the mix. Even here, her activity was infused with no novelty. Saturday was reserved for errands: groceries, a visit from a uniformed technician arriving in a repair van, sweeping her immaculate walk, and re-tying the frayed jute twine that wrapped shrubs, bracing them from a destructive winter prairie wind. Saturdays were homage to the redundant. And Sundays were unknown, for it was impossible to escape our own family routines to spy on the routine of another. Presumably her Sundays were like our own. In any case, the shops of a Mr. Carruthers were never opened on a Sunday, which limited the scope — at least on that one day — for her more criminal activity.

The strength of personality can stamp a routine when that routine is chiselled from the choices one makes. The routine of my life, on the other hand, came from the strength of the personalities of others, above all Walter and Macy, who were responsible for my welfare and my well-being, although they had begun to suspect that I was starting to seize the wheels and cogs that turned my life. But of Mrs. Phillips, too, who ordered the hours of my life from 8:30 each weekday morning until 3:30 each winter afternoon. Observing Mrs. Phillips, I began to wonder what my own routine would reveal were I to choose it freely. Since I had never claimed responsibility for it, and since it had been fashioned by the will of others to which my only duty, until now, was conformity, I had never questioned it. But suddenly a stirring within arose that was quite uncomfortable. An abyss of responsibility yawned before me.

The strength of a routine chiselled entirely from the rock of one's own personality contains also the almost invisible fissure of its own weakness. The structure was sound as long as one ignored the illusion of self-control. Until now, the solidity of my life was borrowed from the control that others exerted over me, however legitimately. I had very little control. My personality existed in a state too unformed as yet to lend strength. A child has no pretension to control. From time to time, it is true, I might rail at submitting to the order imposed by others, but I had not yet discerned the need to impose order from within myself. The silent and internal awakening that would dawn one day can be brutal and unhappy for all who had been responsible for my young life until that moment. But once that dawn began to shine, its light, irreversible, would efface the shadows my young life had mistaken for its own brilliance.

Mrs. Phillips had broken the solid structure of her routine by a random and capricious act that smashed also the predictability of my own life. I was launched into the abyss of responsibility for the trust my unknown ancestor had placed in me. He had hidden a thing of great value for me to discover and reveal. Now it had been wrested from my possession, and my rightful inheritance robbed. I could rely on no super-hero to swoop down into my world and restore justice. It was up to me to reclaim what was mine. The only way to prove the forgery was to restore at the same time what had been lost.

If, as we suspected, Mrs. Phillips would look for a mediator who would pose on her behalf as someone interested in selling what was mine, then she would have to meet that person during the moments of her routine that were not already occupied with legitimate activity. Looking at the results of our surveillance, this left the most probable occasion as a Thursday evening. But I needed to get from probability to certainty. And therein lay my difficulty.

Mr. Carruthers had surprised us by his museum, or rather, his private gallery that housed his own personal collection. He had revealed himself in his actions, too. He had let Tom, Leese, and me into the sphere of his own passions, counted us worthy to stand in the heart of his affections. An invisible threshold had been crossed by his invitation, and our relationship had been altered. It was the first time anyone had done this for me, to call me from my childhood.

A few weeks after our last visit to his shop, and having now completed surveillance of Mrs. Phillips, Tom, Leese, and I together boarded the city bus in the chilly after-school twilight and travelled back to Mr. Carruthers' shop. The faded ribbon and tinkling of the bell as we entered the dusty room sent a thrill down my spine, in the knowledge that more was here than a few tokens displayed for amateur enthusiasts.

I had no particular motive to visit the shop. In fact, I had not come to visit the shop at all. I realized as I entered through the door that I had come to visit with Mr. Carruthers. He greeted us again with a smile that pierced through his heavy eyeglass lenses.

"Come in, come in," he beckoned. "It's taken a nasty chill outside." And indeed it had. We were outfitted in full winter kit. "Close the door quickly."

Tom walked up to the wood and glass display case where Mr. Carruthers had taken his usual place. Tom wasn't interested in stamps, and Tom was not one to pretend to what he was not. "Mr. Carruthers, we have a problem." Leese and I looked sharply at him. Surely he would not reveal the forgery in so unprepared a manner.

"How can someone sell a stamp without anyone knowing the person who is selling it and without anyone else but the buyer and seller knowing what is being sold?"

Mr. Carruthers hesitated a moment, puzzled. "You mean, how could one sell a stamp anonymously? That's a tricky proposition. We talked about that. To shield one's identity in a sale one needs to go through a middle party. But how to shield also the knowledge of what is being sold from that middle party, well, I don't see how it can be done. To sell something on behalf of someone else, one still has to know what one is selling." He looked at Tom, who realized suddenly what he had done.

"We were just wondering. Some people seem to go to a lot of trouble for paintings and stamps and things."

"Yes, they do. Traders act as middle parties to help protect the identity of buyers and sellers, but they know the thing they are trading. They know its value because they know what it is."

The early evening had set in. We could see nothing outside the store windows, although everyone passing by could see us within the dimly lit shop. The overhead light seemed to struggle against the encroaching night and the outdoor sounds were muted, hesitating. The bright tinkle of the bell on the door was shrill and unwelcome. It shocked us. Just a few minutes before closing, someone had come in. A rush of cold brushed over us as a well-wrapped client stood bundled at the door, faltering in the light that, although dim, contrasted with the obscurity out on the street. The person made no attempt to remove winter gloves or push down the fur-lined cowl that hid their face. Eyes peered at us and shone out from a black space.

"Is there a Mr. Carruthers here?" It was a woman's voice, but low and unfeminine. A trace of steel that tapped out "t" and "c." She was speaking to no one in particular.

"I am he."

"Ah," was the only reply. Then, after a prolonged glance around the room, taking the three of us in, she asked, "Do you have a moment?"

"I normally close in ten minutes, but if there is something urgent…?"

"Not urgent, exactly." The client began to unwrap herself. "Pressing."

"I see. Will it take long to explain?"

"I don't believe it will." She looked around at us again while she continued to unwind a long scarf that was wrapped against her throat. "But it is something that demands a certain discretion." The eyes gleamed like tiny chrome orbs that reflected all light without capturing any for themselves.

Mr. Carruthers looked into the eyes, and then looked our way. Leese read the message in his glance. "We need to be getting back." Mr. Carruthers said nothing, but his nothing spoke a word of acknowledgment.

The client continued to divest the layers piled against a winter chill. It was cold, but not quite winter — at least not to us. Her heavy embalming belied that she was unused to our late fall winds. And now that I thought about it, the strange, metallic staccato of her speech might have been the influence of a foreign accent. If she was not a native, then she must have lived here a long time, yet not so long as to completely lose the trace of her origins or acclimatize herself to our brisk autumn weather. But still, long enough that the origins were thoroughly obscured by her almost-local lilt.

She looked into Mr. Carruthers' glass display case. It was placed there for amateurs, with curiosities arranged to incite enthusiasm but nothing there to catch the interest of the serious collector. The woman found nothing in the display to halt her gaze. She looked over her shoulder as the three of us shuffled towards the door, postponing our departure ever so slightly. There was something tantalizingly unusual in this intruder, but it was clear she would say nothing while we were still present. She waited patiently, used to biding her time until the little events of a moment settled in her favour. In the meantime, she removed the hood that obscured her face and turned back to us for reassurance that we were on our way out. Leese held the door open and then she and Tom lighted into the evening street. I started when I saw her face and stood in incomprehension. The face was that of Mrs. Phillips' mother, who arrived precisely at 5:00 each Tuesday evening.

CHAPTER FIFTEEN

———◦·✦·◦———

"So it's not her mother, then," concluded Tom. "Unless Mrs. Phillips sent her mother on a mission." He meant it as a joke.

"It could still be her mother," Leese said without humour. "People do strange things."

"Hrmph."

"None of this is making any sense," I said. "This just isn't like her."

"Neither was stealing your stamp," Tom stated.

"Well, unless she stole on impulse," Leese countered.

"Mrs. Phillips just doesn't do 'random.'" I was trying to connect the dots to form a pattern.

"But she did. So she does," was all Tom could conclude.

"Okay." I was still trying to put it all together, but without success. There had to be a thread of premeditation somewhere here. "How would she find someone who would help her? Where would she look?"

"She'd go to a collector's store."

"But there aren't many of them. I'm sure most would not be as serious as Mr. Carruthers. For him, it's more than just a business. How would she know she could trust them to help her sell a stolen stamp and not turn her in?"

"She'd look around for a shady dealer."

"If I wanted to find a shady dealer, where would I look?"

Leese thought for a moment and then seemed to struggle with an idea. She began slowly, "Maybe there were stories in newspapers about the discovery of a stamp. She'd research them to see if maybe the discovery was strange. Unexplained. I mean, how maybe a lost stamp came into the person's possession."

Not much to go on, but, still, it was a lead.

"So how do you go about finding newspaper articles? There must be thousands of articles and almost none of them are about stamps." I started to feel helpless again. Up until then, research meant looking up entries in the encyclopedia at home. I avoided it as much as possible. If there was no entry in the encyclopedia, it simply didn't exist.

"She would have to narrow her search," Tom said, which I found surprising. But maybe the science guy *should* know more about research techniques than the guy who was satisfied with solving the conundrums of simple mathematics.

"Or have someone help her, guide her in her research," Leese added. "The public library has people who do that, I think. Anyway, someone said they did." So we decided to go to the main library to see what we could do.

The library was in the centre of the city, not far from the river that chiselled a gorge through the urban landscape. In times past a streetcar connected the two banks across an iron bridge that now struggled against rust and the rush of motorized life. By contrast, the library was a thoroughly modern affair, proud of its originality, and efficient. We walked through an immense glass atrium that assured a summer climate despite the approaching gloom of winter outside. A rush of water cascaded down a wall and splashed into pools that formed shallow fountains. Comfortable chairs and benches invited guests to repose in the seasonless hall and enter into the realm of the imaginary and timeless.

It took some time to find the section of the library devoted to the ephemeral dramas that are chronicled in daily newspapers. It was located in a quiet back corner along a bank of windows that streamed in daylight as long as it lasted. Long rows of tables skirted the central circular desk that surveyed the tables. No patrons were seated, and a single librarian sat at the desk, reading. He was a smallish man, immersed in the newspaper spread out before him. Otherwise, the counter, hidden from view at a distance, was perfectly empty and perfectly spotless. He looked up as we approached and gave a perfunctory smile, which was still somehow inviting.

"May I help you?"

"We're looking for some articles," began Leese, pre-empting Tom's advance. "Articles on stamp collecting. On rare stamps that have been found or sold."

The librarian looked directly at her and ignored Tom and myself. "And how far back do you want to check?"

Leese was lost here and opened her mouth without a sound.

"That's interesting," the librarian reflected. "There was a lady here a little while ago who was looking for just that same sort of information. It took a while to put together the results, but she seemed satisfied."

It seemed incredible that Mrs. Phillips would come here for exactly the same purpose. "How long ago was she here?" I asked.

"At least a month ago." The man twisted slightly to a keyboard embedded in the countertop and quickly keyed in some terms. A screen was also embedded in the clean countertop and he waited as the results started appearing.

"Well," I continued, "we're working on a school project about stamps and their importance."

"The search has been saved and I've just called it up. Would you like to see it?"

"That would be great," Tom burst in. "Great luck!"

A printer whirred from somewhere beneath the contours of the desk. The librarian glanced over the pages and arranged them in some order. "There weren't very many results. They cover the last five years." He handed them over to us and I began sifting through them. He observed me as I glanced over the headlines. At one particular article he interrupted me and pointed to it. "She seemed particularly interested in this one, if I recall." The article was about the sale of an extremely valuable stamp. It had a photo placed in the article. Two women stared out at us with wide grins. One was the lady from the shop.

"Bingo," Tom said.

The librarian continued to stare.

"Great luck!" Tom said again.

I gathered up the articles, paid the small sum required, and we turned and left. It would have been pleasant to sit at the long tables and peruse our "find" under the warm stream of sunshine, but we were too excited to contain ourselves to whispers under the watchful gaze of a librarian. A little celebration was in order.

Near the cascading water was a small coffee shop serving real hot chocolate. Sitting at an entirely glass table we scrutinized the article. It was about a rare find, a first-issue colonial stamp of Vancouver Island. My queen now looked older and rounder, more regal and more resolved. She was traced in faded dusty rose. There were no perforations on the stamp, suggesting that it was a trial issue. The British North American colony was then only recently established, cut off from the rest of the country by its Pacific location off the mainland, and six thousand kilometres away from the Eastern Canadian colonies that were already in talks to unite under one dominion. Long stretches of grasslands and prairie, which I now inhabited, and ranges of formidable mountain chains cut off the western colonies from the east. For a century and a half, man had utterly defied geography to link east and west. The stamp was a first foray to test the needs of the determined settlers in a hesitant settlement.

The article speculated that the value of the unusual find could be four times what my Penny Black was thought to fetch. The article indicated it had been circulating at regional fairs and generating a great deal of excitement. A brief caption under the image of the stamp revealed that it was in the custody of Lana White on behalf of an anonymous collector: White to cherish dusty rose.

White to sell my Penny Black.

The next day we were sounding the little bell as we entered Mr. Carruthers' storefront, again with no clear strategy about what to do or say but there seemed nowhere else to go to seek answers. It was colder and the autumn weather had shed its pretensions and turned to winter. A dull sky, grey-white even without clouds, hung high above the centretown business towers in the distance. Daylight in this winter sky was not a stream irradiating from a distant star, but a sort of clear fog that invaded every space while concealing its source, impenetrable in its opaque clarity, but filling every crevice with a milky luminosity. Vapour rose from invisible metal heating vents off the tops of commercial buildings, rising in straight, wispy columns undisturbed by the breath of any breeze. A winter stillness clung in the cold, clear air.

The tinkle of the little bell seemed shocking in contrast as we swung open the front door, frosted from the humidity and heat. And it was welcomingly warm inside. I shivered, and as I always did when I entered, I glanced around. Even though I knew every book on the few shelves, I was still impelled to quickly seek out my bearings in the tiny shopfront, which always seemed like crossing a threshold of time.

But this time there was something different. Mr. Carruthers was absent, not merely hidden in the streams of dusted light. Indeed, the dull outside light cast no distinct rays for the dust to appear in the air and shield his presence. It was impossible for the owner to conjure up his presence in these conditions. He was either there, or not there.

Not there, apparently. But he had left a mark. A book stood open on his glass display case. I went closer in curiosity. It was unlike Mr. Carruthers to leave anything about. I dared not touch the book nor swing it round to see it full on. Instead, I read the upside-down page. The open leaf described a portion of British colonial philatelic history, in particular, the newly founded British North America Crown colony of British Columbia and a list of Vancouver Island stamps. The dusty rose cameo of a plump Queen Victoria was listed amongst others.

From within the back of the shop I heard a door quietly shut and Mr. Carruthers appeared shortly afterwards. He had been in his "museum." With a client? With Lana White?

"Ahh," was all he said. He seemed distracted and his hair was slightly dishevelled on top as if he had been pulling at it. His eyes retreated behind the thick lenses and shut out his thoughts. Tom and Leese were pretending to look at a couple of books from the shelves. He cast his eyes down at the book that lay open on his glass and wooden case. He stared at it for a moment, as if recollecting what it was about. We remained silent in the face of his unusual distraction. He was not a distracted person. Usually he was very focused, inscrutable but concentrated. He took things in but let little pass to the world from his own interior activity. The exception had been our last visit when he showed us into the surprising gallery from where he had just come. We had been invited into his world and thoughts. He would not shut us out now.

I was unsure how to begin. Again, I felt the need not to arouse suspicion, but I was guileless and hopeless at dissembling my real thoughts and intentions. Not that I was focused like he was, at least not until recently, but now something from the world outside had touched me, affected me. I could no longer stand as a passive object to which events simply happened. Everything had changed in my world. I decided at that moment, without the least hesitation or forethought, that the confidence Mr. Carruthers had bestowed on me needed like payment in return.

I pointed to the dusty rose queen. "Lana White last sold that stamp."

Mr. Carruthers blinked at me and remained silent. Then he looked down at the book. "It was sold six weeks ago."

"From an anonymous seller to an unnamed buyer," I said. He continued to look at the book. "By Lana White."

He looked up at me quickly. He had dropped his inscrutable façade but changed no outward expression. Only his eyes pierced through his glasses once again.

"She was the woman in here yesterday," I added.

Mr. Carruthers started. "Mrs. Lina Feher," he said. "She was the woman who asked to see me yesterday."

"Oh." I was crushed.

He continued to look straight at me without saying anything. Then, after what seemed a very long silence, he added, "Feher is the Hungarian word for 'white.'"

Tom stood beside me, and I could feel Leese breathing on my neck.

"And the woman yesterday was Hungarian?" Tom guessed.

"A very long time ago," Mr. Carruthers said. "She moved here many years ago. I recognized her from several philatelic trading shows. She is very knowledgeable."

I took out the newspaper article that was folded in my pocket. All Mr. Carruthers said upon seeing it was, "Yes." He closed the book on the counter and looked at all three of us. "I have only ever had one dealing with her. It was a long time ago and I was still young. It is not a happy memory."

"Was it about that collector you were talking about the other day?" Tom asked.

"Yes. Not so much a collector, as I said, but one who was obsessed with possessing rare and unattainable things. I was able to contact the owner of the stamp he wanted, but what I did not say was that I never actually met the owner. He wanted to remain anonymous so I had to work through an agent. Lina Feher — Lana White. She's very good at what she does. She thought I did not remember her yesterday, and I did not disabuse her of her erroneous assumption. She took a risk, no doubt, in coming here, but that is what she does. Her success has been achieved by taking deliberate and calculated risks."

"What was she looking for?" Leese finally interjected. "Why would she contact you and not tell you her real name?"

Mr. Carruthers thought for a moment. "Identities are curious things. An identity depends on the trust we place in the person who asserts it. Most of all, however, an identity depends on the understanding we attain of *ourselves* — or, sadly, on our capacity to *deceive* ourselves. Our capacity to deceive others, too, and so mask who we are." He stopped again.

"Ivan the Giant," I whispered almost inaudibly. It wasn't a name I liked and I had never before spoken it aloud. Neither Tom nor Leese had ever called me that. I had never asserted that name and never encouraged others to call me that. One day I would just be Ivan again, when others caught up to my untimely period of growth, but already I was still just "Ivan" to myself and to my best friends, as I always had been to Walter and Macy. No one else could make me assume an identity invented for me. For her part, Leese had been endowed with an unfortunate last name, Troll, that could have caused her an unhappy life amongst unthinking and unconsciously cruel classmates, but she never paid attention to their taunts nor entered into their game. The giant and the troll were the inventions of others. Tom was Tom and he took us for Ivan and Leese. As did Mr. Carruthers.

"She wants me to believe she is not who she is. But *she* knows perfectly well who she is. It's just that who she *is*, in fact, is inconvenient for her at the present. And so, she assumes another identity. But the trust was broken long ago, and so the deception fails.

"She asked if I knew of anyone interested in trading something of value." Mr. Carruthers continued at last, looking full on at me and blinking, but by now I understood his glance and I did not find it uncomfortable. He was processing something that required a brief space of time to put in order before it could be communicated appropriately. "She asked if I knew anyone who had anything of interest to sell."

Mr. Carruthers stopped there. After a moment, Tom asked, "And do you, Mr. Carruthers?"

"I don't know, Tom. What do you think?" But Mr. Carruthers was not looking at Tom, he was looking up at me, Ivan, who stared back at him, from a position a little above his head.

More trust was being asked of me, and I knew it.

"There is a problem," I heard myself say. No one spoke. Leese and Tom stared at me. I recognized that a moment had arrived which had to be either seized with all its consequences, or passed over and abandoned completely. But passing over also had its consequences. I would remain the bearer of a fraudulent stamp, I would renege on the trust my great-grandfather had placed in me, and I would bow to a hastily devised deception that robbed me of an inheritance. But most of all, it suddenly occurred to me, I would fail myself.

To reveal my suspicions now meant at the same time trusting in the one person who could verify them, and trusting also that he was not deceiving me; that he was who he said he was, that he did what he said he did, and that he did not do what he did not claim to do. It was my suspicion which was making a claim that now needed to be either proved or disproved, but there was no way to attain the proof without trusting in the one who might also be caught up in the deception, or at least using it for his own profit.

"I never actually found the stamp I lost."

CHAPTER SIXTEEN

———◆⬥◆———

Mrs. Phillips proved to be as distracted as Mr. Carruthers had been at the beginning of our visit to his shop the previous day. She did not even check her attendance folder. She confused the first period's plan with the second and tapped her finger restlessly against her desktop all day. She did not seem to see any of us, she ignored our questions or answered what had not been asked, and she even allowed Tom to walk about the room when he had no reason to get up. Her restlessness was communicated directly to us and we shifted tiresomely in our desks and fidgeted with papers and books when we should have been reading or working. It was a beautiful, sunny, and bitterly cold day.

Mr. Carruthers had contacted Walter and after school we were to go over to the bank to examine the stamp, which I had explained was probably a quickly devised fake because it contained no remnants of the ancient adhesive on the reverse side. Mr. Carruthers would be able to make a more expert appraisal. My father had listened on the telephone in complete silence. He had nothing to add because he had no expertise by which to question the procedure or doubt the assertions. After he hung up, he looked into my eyes and placed his hand briefly on the top of my head, exerting a light and sympathetic pressure. He was still taller than I, a large and vigorous human being.

We met Mr. Carruthers at the bank. He had brought with him a special box, perfectly formed as a cube fitting in the palm of his hand, of polished ebony. When he finally opened it to receive the stamp, I saw it was lined with a fine, red sheen. "Silk," he said. "If stored carefully, it resists mold and is not prey to dust mites. The clever invention of a humble worm."

We drove back to his shop and he led us wordlessly to the back room. Again, I heard the quiet whirr of smooth-fitted bolts as they slid in their hidden sleeves when Mr. Carruthers placed his fingers on the door handle. He gently turned counter-clockwise as he looked up into my father's eyes. "It is a secure room, as secure as any safe. This is an extra precaution, a left-twist of the wrist instead of the usual right to open the door." He tapped very lightly the two polished steel buttons on the door jamb, indicating the exposed end of recessed bolts that slid from the door jamb into the door when it was locked, much as the door of a safe, but more discreet.

Once again, a perimeter of light emitted slowly from the bottom circumference of the room as the door was opened, and the shimmering whiteness within revealed itself gradually upwards in a soft glow. No direct source of light could be seen anywhere, and no shadows were cast, not even by the lone circle of a table in the centre.

Walter seemed awed, as I had been the first time I entered here. The contrast with the dusty light of the front shop could not be greater. Mr. Carruthers walked up to the round table and placed the perfectly formed ebony cube on the shiny white surface, precisely in the middle, staring at it for a moment. Before opening it, he turned to my father and explained all that he had already revealed to me. In a sense, this was his true habitat, not the storefront. Just as his thick eye-glasses seemed to obscure his eyes only to reveal them when he made a pointed inquiry, so the small, wood-lined store entrance obscured the real business that was carried on in this room. Here transactions were completed, significant trades negotiated, and investigations undertaken. Our purpose here was the latter, an investigation. Opening the shiny box, he brought out a delicate pair of soft tweezers from an unobserved and incredibly narrow drawer under the table. He picked up the stamp and looked closely at it, turning its back to his gaze.

"Incredibly fine work. The quality of the paper is the chief means of deception and leads one to conclude the originality of the print." He withdrew a large magnifying glass from the same hidden drawer. "The printing technique is not extraordinary, but sufficient to deceive in the circumstances. Nevertheless, when one examines with a little more care, one can note that the tiny pin-pricks of ink used to create the image in the technique of the time are not well-executed. A very high-resolution photocopier has been used." He twirled the image around and held it upwards for a moment while examining it. "But it was a copier just the same. In the time when this stamp was printed, a different, more primitive technology was used. The colour would be less evenly distributed. This forgery was produced quickly, on the spur of the moment, but still with some skill and forethought. It was designed to replicate with sufficient authenticity for the purposes at hand, and it had chiefly two factors in favour of dissimulation: first, that the remaining mint-condition originals are so rare that few persons have ever examined them closely and, secondly, that it was meant to deceive children and the inexpert." Here he looked at me, and then up at Walter. "It might have been successful," he continued as he turned to examine again the reverse side of the stamp, "had the person not reckoned on the proficiency of your brief apprenticeship, Ivan." He paused, then without looking at me added, "You are exactly right. The real failing of replication is to have overlooked the need to also deceive the actual 'feel' of the thing, the slightly uneven surface of the old gum." He smiled.

Thus encouraged, I decided to articulate my own conclusions. "I think..." I hesitated. Mr. Carruthers blinked at me so as to signal confidence. "The person thinks they have been... successful. But they also know that the forgery will be easy enough to detect. They will want to get rid of the original as quickly as possible so it's not found on them." Mr. Carruthers blinked again. "And they will want to get rid of it without anyone knowing who it is that is getting rid of it. They won't want anyone to be able to trace the original back to them."

"They will want an anonymous transaction," Mr. Carruthers completed my thought.

"Exactly. That's why that lady was in the shop asking you if anyone had something to sell."

"I have been thinking the same thing. But why ask me if someone I know has something to *sell*? You only have a forgery — a fake — to sell, and she doesn't know that I am aware of that. Doesn't the thief actually want to find a *buyer* for her — for their — authentic stamp? At first, the lady's question made no sense to me. She should have asked if I knew of a *buyer*. But then, upon reflection, I thought perhaps there is a plan, a rather devious strategy. Let us hypothesize for a moment. Let us say that I tell Mrs. Lina Feher — I'll use the name she gave me recently, for all I know it is her true name — let us say that I tell her that I *do* have someone who wants to sell something of great value. Let us say I tell her you wish to sell, but, of course, I do not tell her who you are. The discretion of all parties is of the utmost importance in such transactions. This would be nothing unusual. Nor would it be unusual for her to conceal her own client — her fictitious client — who wishes to buy." Walter fidgeted. We were both getting lost. True, it made no sense that Lina Feher was looking for me to *sell* my stamp. If she were truly working for Mrs. Phillips, Mrs. Phillips would know my stamp was a fake and would not be offering to buy it. But Mrs. Feher had quite pointedly asked if I would sell my stamp.

Mr. Carruthers seemed to sense our puzzlement. "But why ask if I knew of anyone — that is to say, if you, Ivan — would be willing to *sell* your stamp? Mrs. Phillips would certainly know the replica in your possession is worthless, even if Mrs. Feher is ignorant of the theft and forgery. Should it not make greater sense for her to have asked if I know of any clients — not you, Ivan, but one of my wealthy contacts — who might be interested in buying your stamp, which is now in her possession? She would anonymously remove the evidence from any trace to her own person and collect a substantial sum as well." Mr. Carruthers looked at both of us. "Hers was a curious question in the circumstances. Do you not think so, Ivan?"

I could see his point. Then it struck me. "But what if her intention — at least at this point — is not to get rid of the original. What if her intention is something else?"

Mr. Carruthers smiled. "Yes, Ivan, and what would that intention be?"

"What if she wanted to publicly prove that the stamp I now have is actually not authentic? Her intent was to…" I hesitated, not sure how to express it.

Mr. Carruthers articulated the thought. "Her intention is to divert any form of suspicion from herself. Everyone thinks you have found the stamp you had lost. She alone knows that what you found is her copy. At this point she does not know that you suspect that it is not the original stamp your great-grandfather hid. All she has to do is show to everyone — show the world — that what you think is an authentic and valuable discovery is, in fact, inauthentic and valueless. No one knows that the original was stolen. She has no need to cast suspicion *from* herself, because, in fact, no one suspects her. No one except you, Ivan."

"And you," I said. "Now you suspect her too, don't you?" I needed reassurance from Mr. Carruthers that I was not inventing a tale.

Mr. Carruthers simply smiled. "What you have said makes sense. Her plan is very simple indeed. It is to have me confirm that what is in your possession is not an authentic Penny Black. She knows this will be evident the moment you agree to sell your stamp and I have a chance to mediate the transaction. I will be the unwitting instrument facilitating the fulfilment of her plan. Her plan is to gain time by having us all think our original excitement over your discovery was misplaced, and then to sell the real Penny Black, now quietly in her possession, when this whole incident is forgotten."

"It seems so simple," Walter said.

"Ingenious in its simplicity," Mr. Carruthers added.

"Leese says the simplest plans are usually the best because they have the least that can go wrong," I said.

Mr. Carruthers looked up again at Walter and me. "That is true. But I have been thinking. There might be a solution, also simple in its own way. It is to appeal to her primary motive."

"I'm not sure I follow," Walter said.

"You see, her *immediate* motive is to remove any chance of suspicion falling on her, assuming she is the one who produced the forgery and set you up to find it, Ivan. But that is not her *primary* motive. She is not a collector. She was bequeathed a collection from her brother and she was quite willing to sell off any items of even moderate value," he turned to me, "which you now possess, Ivan. You have the only two items of worth in that collection. She had no interest in holding on to them, whether out of interest in philately or out of sentimental affection for her deceased brother. She directed me to sell what I could. Her primary motive in all of this strategy, therefore, cannot be to hold on to the authentic Penny Black. Her primary motive for the theft has always been to profit by it, and so to sell the stamp. I need only appeal to that primary motive and bypass the subterfuge."

I was not following and my face must have showed it. "Instead of saying I had someone who wanted to sell something of value — you, Ivan — what if I answered that I have someone who wished to *buy* something of value?"

"But I can't afford to buy the stamp," Walter interrupted.

"No, and I would not expect you to. In fact, I would not expect anyone to actually buy it. The goal is to deploy subterfuge in return for subterfuge, to use the same strategy on her that she is using on us. I do not relish playing the role of a hapless intermediary who is duped into facilitating base thievery, but I don't mind the role of mediator who puts things right."

Mr. Carruthers obviously had a plan, but I was not entirely following, nor, from what I could gather, was my father. We discussed it further until I could grasp the outlines of the strategy. It still seemed risky to me, but better than the certainty of having my credibility crushed by confirming that what was in my possession was not authentic, with the implication that it never had been, that my great-grandfather was himself duped. Somehow, even more than the risk of losing forever the treasure that was given to me, the thought of playing into the hands of a thief seemed a betrayal to my great-grandfather who obviously knew that what he had found was of significance and value, and who trusted his descendant to be intelligent enough to put faith in his confidence.

Walter and Mr. Carruthers were agreed, and so the counter-strategy was accepted. I could only sit on the sidelines and watch it unfold. Mr. Carruthers kept the forged stamp. It was worthless anyway and a reminder of what had been lost. I would not be an actor in the next phase of the drama as it was decided that, since my identity seemed unknown to Mrs. Lina Feher, it was best to keep it that way and not risk her seeing me again. Mr. Carruthers would handle all the arrangements, and if I was not mistaken, his eyes sparkled. Having once been the naïve pawn in one of Mrs. Feher-White's games, he relished the chance now to outwit her.

* * *

A few weeks later, Mr. Carruthers invited Walter and me into the security of his white vault and told his story. He had informed Mrs. Lina Feher that he did not find anyone wishing to sell anything of interest at that time. He said that he did, in fact, know one person who had something of particular value, but they were not ready to part with it just yet. On the other hand, while making his inquiries on her behalf, he explained to her that he received notice from one serious philatelist that he wished to add to his holdings. His interest was in British Commonwealth issue. The person in question was personally known to Mr. Carruthers and they had engaged in successful transactions on previous occasions. The person was discreet and wished to remain anonymous, as Mrs. Feher herself could understand. She nodded slightly, closing her eyes in perfect agreement, and assuring Mr. Carruthers that her own clients usually solicited the same discretion. It was safer all around for all parties, of course. Mr. Carruthers assured her of his perfect discretion.

Mrs. Feher took time to consult with persons, she said, who often asked her to mediate their transactions. She reported back that she had "one or two" who showed some interest. That "one in particular" was ready to enter into discussions to see what might be done, but that the client had a particular concern. Here Mrs. Feher hesitated, unsure how to proceed. Mr. Carruthers blinked in a perfectly non-committal but inviting way.

"It seems the person has come into possession of the item in an unexpected way." Mrs. Feher's metallic t's were softened on the sibilant s's of her slight foreign accent.

Mr. Carruthers remained silent, feigning incomprehension.

"That is to say, the client had not been deliberately pursuing any specific acquisition, when it… well, when circumstances presented themselves in such a way, that, in fact…" here she faltered.

To which Mr. Carruthers let out a hurried gust, "Oh, yes, I see." His assurance that "discretion is of the highest order" at first startled then reassured Mrs. Feher. She smiled with unnaturally white teeth and retreating eyes. "The greatest acquisitions often arise through unforeseen means. It is what gives them their charm and their interest." Mr. Carruthers peered into the face of Mrs. Feher, veiled with wrinkles of smile about her lips and cheeks, while calculations carried on behind the oddly cold pretense of warmth and intimacy. It was just the tactic she had last used on him when he was too young and inexperienced to recognize it as a ploy to invite a confidence that would be exploited but never repaid. "I can assure you, Mrs. Feher, that my client is entirely familiar with all lines of inquiry and all methods of acquisition." The machinations behind the smile continued. A doubt lingered, and he began to wonder if she recalled their other transaction when he had refused to engage in underhanded methods to satisfy a client's competitive obsession. She obviously had recognized him or she would not have employed the ruse of a false name. Or perhaps it was her original name in her native language, and she had adopted "White" simply to move more easily within the circles she targeted. "I can assure you of my own perfect discretion as well. I have now been at these matters some time. I have handled all types of transactions for all manner of… persons." He could see that he had directly struck at the precise point of her uncertainty and had resolved her lingering doubt. "Mine is not so much the role of merchant, you see, as that of mediator. The responsibility for the niceties of the transactions lies with the parties. My place is to facilitate a… uhhhh, resolution… desired by each of the parties."

"Exactly my attitude, Mr. Carruthers. I see we approach our delicate task in like fashion." She smiled in earnest now. "So reassuring." Mr. Carruthers smiled back and nodded very slightly.

So, a time was arranged to finalize the details. But first Mr. Carruthers quietly demanded that the stamp that was to be exchanged, of which neither he nor Mrs. Feher spoke, must first be authenticated. This posed a problem because it was evident that Mrs. Feher had no idea what the stamp was that her "client" had wished to sell, as the client was adamant from the beginning that the "item of transfer" itself be unknown "to those entrusted with the mediation." Mr. Carruthers offered a solution after restating the very unusual nature of the request. Mrs. Feher shrugged her shoulders.

"We are always dealing with originals, Mr. Carruthers. And not just the stamps themselves." She smiled again.

"Just so." So he proposed that he involve a third party who would independently verify the originality of the stamp and suggest a market price that might serve as a basis for subsequent negotiations. This was all very satisfactory, Mrs. Feher concluded. And the interview ended with another round of counterfeit smiles.

CHAPTER SEVENTEEN

———◆▸◀◆———

Mrs. Phillips proved very indulgent in class during this period. She smiled easily and almost skipped into class each morning. She called Tom "dear" at one moment. Her unaccustomed leniency was abused by the students, who managed to ingratiate themselves easily by returning her smiles. Homework was lightened and lawlessness threatened: whispering and notes, the shuffle of feet under desks, and the occasional unauthorized foray to retrieve some personal item from the shelf that held our individual belongings. Normally, this would have been dismissed with a reminder that we needed to develop the discipline to fetch all necessary books and items at the beginning of the period, and that forgetfulness and lack of foresight for the task at hand would not serve us well in our futures. Now, all was forgiven, or at least overlooked. Something else was on her mind. And I guessed that it was the prospect of great profit from a risk now taken and, seemingly, won.

Leese, in her fashion, was suspicious. Tom was willing to run with the good times until they exhausted themselves.

"What's going on?" Leese asked at lunch one day. It was too cold now to be outside, but the raucous lunch hall afforded discretion behind the tumult of children's voices freed from the constraints of the classroom. She looked at me and repeated, "Do *you* know what's going on?"

I said I thought I did. "I think she might have someone to buy her stamp."

"You mean *your* stamp," Tom said.

"Yes, well…" I explained briefly what had happened and how Mr. Carruthers had a plan. Leese was skeptical but Tom thought it had a chance. It was a plan that required both urgency and caution.

Mrs. Phillips walked through the hall. I saw her from the corner of my eye and tried not to look directly at her. She looked over in my direction and her gaze hovered over me, or so I thought. I had never seen her disturb our lunch time in the years I had been there. Indeed, it was unlike her to mingle in the chaos of students unconstrained beyond the glossy painted cinderblock walls of prepared lessons. Yes, she had fixed her gaze at me. She pursed her lips and, I thought, squinted her eyes. A squall of screams from a table of lunch-time revellers squeezed the air tightly. I decided to look back at Mrs. Phillips. The screams made her wince and my look stunned her. She jolted her head and pressed her shoulders together, striding out of the hall with great purpose.

The afternoon was savage. Gone was the dreamily distracted teacher, returned was the supreme class monitor who let not a single infraction of her invisible rules pass unnoticed. Or unpunished. We were crushed into silence. Questions were not tolerated. Comments were derided. She challenged us into submission and not even Tom dared a gallant attempt to resurrect her humour.

"That was weird," Leese observed as we slunk outdoors after the last jarring bell ended the confinement. I agreed that it was.

"Well, something's happened," was all Tom offered. "That's not like her at all."

"Neither were the last few days," I said. The pattern of behaviour had been interrupted now in both directions, unaccustomed leniency and then unhabitual severity.

"What's happened with Mr. Carruthers?"

"Nothing that I know of."

But something had happened. That evening Walter came home and said we were to go in to see Mr. Carruthers after supper. He'd be waiting for us.

Which he was.

The lights were off in the front shop and my father, after peering in, rapped lightly on the door's window pane, right over the name of the owner, who suddenly appeared from out of the darkness within and led us inside without a single word.

He took us to the vault, and the brightness and controlled temperature made me blink and squint and shiver all at once.

The small black box lined with red silk rested on the shiny white surface of the round table, exactly in the middle. A third chair had been brought in and we all sat down. Mr. Carruthers pushed the box over to me and continued staring at it. I looked up at him.

"Open it, Ivan." Which is what I did.

My great-grandfather's heirloom lay still upon the red silk of the interior. It *was* his, I could tell right away. I don't know how, but I could. The close facsimile, hastily but quite accurately made, was still not identical. It was hard to explain. One could not directly detect the falsity of the copy, but it was registered somewhere in the minute detail perceived by the human eye. I carefully pinched a corner and lifted it up, then turned it around and slid another finger over the surface. The slight roughness of the ancient adhesive was there, and I smiled very slightly.

Mr. Carruthers caught my smile and smiled back.

"There you are," was all he said.

Walter needed confirmation, "So that's the original?" I nodded, and he reached out to touch it as well, brushing my hand ever so slightly.

"It was a tricky affair," Mr. Carruthers continued. "But it worked. I wasn't at all sure that it would, but it did." In a few words, he explained how the clandestine switch occurred, facilitated by Mrs. Phillips' inexperience and Mrs. Feher's — Lana White's — incaution. He was able to switch the stamps, undetected, before they were handed over to the expert for analysis. The expert was given the forgery that Mrs. Phillips had crafted and Mr. Carruthers kept the original. It was easy, in a way, but highly risky. The risk had paid off. He had beaten Lina Feher at her own game and cheated Mrs. Phillips of her fraud. He obviously felt a great satisfaction, not just in righting a wrong, but in compensating for having been taken advantage of in his youthful inexperience. He had changed since then, but perhaps Mrs. Feher had not changed so much. What had worked in her favour in earlier years now became a liability which could be deftly exploited.

"Mrs. Phillips has been advised by a third-party expert that her stamp is not authentic. She has been informed that it is a rather good quality forgery, but a forgery nonetheless. I don't know how she took it, as I was not supposed to know that it was she who had presented it in the first place."

"My great-grandfather would be relieved," I remarked, and Walter gently reached out and stroked the top of my head with his large hand. "Mostly, I felt bad about that."

"How do we thank you?" Walter asked.

"By not losing it again!"

When we arrived home, Walter let me keep the Penny Black, which was reward in itself. We would deposit it in the safety deposit box at the bank early tomorrow, but for now I could possess my stern little queen again. I went up to my room straight away and pulled out Dr. Seuss from my shelf.

> *One fish,*
> *Two fish,*
> *Red fish,*
> *Blue fish.*

"Black fish," I added and tucked her away amidst the child's rhyme.

Mrs. Phillips was waiting for us before the class began and she did not wait for the bell to ring. Tom was late and he was not spared. He had to take his late card to the office and explain his tardiness to the authorities. When he returned, Mrs. Phillips had the cold look of the vanquished bent on revenge. She turned her back to fetch something and Tom looked at Leese and me and raised his shoulders in a silent question, "What's that all about?"

I had to wait until recess to explain, hurriedly and in whispers, what had happened. The Penny Black was by now safely stored away in the bank's own vault, but Mrs. Phillips must have understood by this time that a ruse had been inflicted upon her. Never mind that she had played a ruse on me.

"This isn't going to be good," was all Tom said.

And it wasn't.

I was singled out at every hour for some imperceptible infraction. Once I was sent to the principal's office for something I did not understand and could not explain. Mr. Marjonson, a mild man of limited but useful experience, simply stared. He said he would take it up with my teacher later and I was sent back to the room as mystified as when I had left. We had a spelling quiz that afternoon and it was returned with a grade of two out of ten. I even lost marks for scribbling my answer over the ruled lines of the page. I recalled this as a typographical misdemeanour when I was in grade two and learning to write cursively, but I had not been penalized since then, even if, admittedly, my writing tended to wander across a page rather than align in strictly horizontal spaces. I lost marks for uncrossed t's and incomplete vowels. I passed a surprise math quiz, but just barely. No one else in the class managed three out of ten points. She had deliberately demanded formulations we had not yet covered and answers that we could not give. It infuriated her that I was the only one to pass, but as it was the end of the day, she had no time to invent further humiliations or exact greater retribution. She left the room precisely as the bell was ringing and was gone from the hallway before its echo had subsided.

Everyone slumped, and in a daze put their books away in complete silence. The principal put his head through the door and, unable to comprehend an entirely silent classroom of eleven-year-olds freed for the day, worked his lips silently, looked in my direction, and retreated to the rising din of the hallway.

"That was weird," was all Leese said, again. For once she wasn't very insightful.

Outside it was cold and the bitter wind did not spare us. Bundled up tightly, everyone hurried quickly into the darkening light. Everyone, except me. I had a dull, heavy coat with a hood that zipped into a tunnel around my face, impermeable to the vicious elements and which left me unperceived to any passers-by. I wandered out into the playground, almost impervious to the frightening chill, and found myself turning the corner where Mrs. Phillips lived. I slowed even more when I perceived a car waiting in front of her house, idling and, from the exhaust pipe, sending up a vapour that was caught by the wind and dispersed into the evening glow. When a prairie winter hits its stride, the vapour in the air freezes and the empty spaces between all things sparkle and shimmer as the wan light passes through. Infinitesimal prisms of frozen humidity separate the light that seems suspended now in what one thought was a void. The dry snow piled underfoot dampens the sounds so that the world seems emptied of moving things, filled only with the unexpected inertia of all that goes unnoticed in more hospitable seasons. A thief could steal up behind without a sound.

Mrs. Phillips stole out of her house and almost ran through the air to the car, flinging open the door and landing in the passenger seat. It was the "Tuesday" car, the car I now knew to be Mrs. Lana White's — or Lina Feher's, whoever she really was. The car jumped too, it seemed, and silently sped by. I could just make out the two of them sitting within as I remained invisible in my hooded hide-away. They would plan a counter-move to Mr. Carruthers' subtle deception. Or would they? Did Mrs. Lina Feher know that the stamp was mine? Would Mrs. Phillips risk revealing her hastily improvised forgery techniques? Only time would tell. More waiting. Like the frozen air hanging in its pale void, "waiting" seemed the almost imperceptible composition of life.

Walter was home early, waiting for me. He had not much to say. The Penny Black was safe this time, authenticated and true. He had seen to it himself first thing that morning, which seemed a lifetime away now. I didn't have much to say either, having been exhausted trying to anticipate Mrs. Phillips' various traps laid throughout the day. I went up to my room to empty my knapsack of the day's contents. My father followed me up after a few moments.

"You could have told me sooner," he said. It was not an accusation, just a statement of fact. "Maybe I could have done something."

I nodded, "I know." Then, "I'm not sure there was anything anyone could have done. Besides, I wasn't sure that the stamp we found wasn't the same one that I lost. I didn't know how to prove it. Who would believe an eleven-year-old?"

"Not many," he agreed. "Me." Then, "Mr. Carruthers, too."

I nodded again. "Thanks."

"You're clever, Ivan." I looked up at him. It was not usual in our family to gush, and its rarity made the compliment more penetrating. He left it at that. Enough father-son bonding for one season.

After a few minutes' silence, during which I rummaged around my room and he stood leaning on the door, I said, "Do you think she'll do anything now? To get the stamp back?"

"It would be foolish of her to try. No one knows she stole it or tried to forge it. It would be a risk to let that out into the public."

"Maybe it was foolish of her to take it in the first place, in a classroom full of kids." Walter was silent. Of course it had been foolish and a great risk. Would she risk again? "All day she was trying to get at me. Like she was picking a fight." I looked at him. "Ex... exacting revenge." Walter blinked at me. "She knows. For sure she knows."

"Well, her fight will be with Mr. Carruthers now, not you."

"Yes, but I'm her target. Every time she looks at me in class she'll be reminded. Her fight might be with Mr. Carruthers, but I'll be the target."

"Do you think you should stay home for a few days? Let her get over it?"

"I don't think Mrs. Phillips gets over anything." I sat on the bed and Walter came and sat beside me. I was almost as tall as he. "No, there's no sense trying to avoid it," I said out loud, but to myself. "I can't do anything about it, but it's no good avoiding it either." Walter looked at me for a long moment.

After supper the front doorbell rang and Tom and Leese came in. I explained to Macy and Walter that they knew everything. We sat in the room adjoining the kitchen. Tom sprawled on the floor with Leese sitting tightly on the edge of a sofa, her feet just touching the ground. My mother made some hot chocolate to warm cheeks reddened by the winter cold. Tom murmured polite appreciation and Leese precisely articulated her thanks without, somehow, sounding rehearsed or artificial. We went over the events again, but with a view to developing a strategy so as to meet tomorrow's expected aggression from our grade six teacher. Walter sat at the kitchen table with Macy, listening but not intervening. Tom and Leese were at complete ease in front of my parents. There was space for everyone to speak.

We tried to think of a way to introduce distractions in class if things followed an uncomfortable trajectory, but we all knew that Mrs. Phillips was too disciplined to be easily thwarted from her intentions. Leese thought we should shift away from distractions altogether. She thought the better strategy would be to play up to the teacher in Mrs. Phillips. If, as happened today, Mrs. Phillips showed signs of covering the subject-matter beyond our capacities, we should follow up with polite interjections designed to show interest, and so force her to explain. In other words, force her to be more exacting in what was, after all, her own strength: teaching and explanation. This sounded like an approach that might work, and so we discussed the classes we would have the next day, and mentally tried to anticipate the areas where we might make judicious inquiries that would lead her to elaborate on the subjects we were meant to cover. It was distraction of a kind, but one which played into her penchant for detail and precision. Walter sipped his hot chocolate.

"But, you know," Leese added as we were wrapping up our strategy session, "Mrs. Phillips hasn't been predictable throughout this whole thing. We shouldn't be surprised if she does something unexpected again. Something that even she hasn't thought of ahead of time."

"Well, that's not very helpful, Leese," was all Tom said.

"But Leese is right. What if Mrs. Phillips decides to take a risk again?"

"Like what?"

"That's the point. We won't know before she does. And neither will she."

"In that case, there's no use talking about it and planning for it."

"Not exactly," I said. I wasn't sure what I really was getting at, but there was a nagging feeling in my mind that the erratic behaviour of Mrs. Phillips was actually something that might be anticipated, strange as that seemed. "Mrs. Phillips always has a plan. She always thinks everything through. She knows exactly what we're going to do for each minute of every day. That's her strength. But that's also her weakness. When something suddenly comes up that she hasn't planned for, she reacts out of character and in a really risky way that puts herself in danger."

"So far she's managed her risks pretty well. It took Carruthers to dream up a way to foil her plan," Leese said.

"Yes, but Mr. Carruthers is a planner, too," I replied. "When he takes a risk, he plans it carefully." Then I added, "But I'm not like that. I'm not a planner." I stopped for a moment. My short life passed before my eyes. "I've just sort of fallen in with whatever happens."

"Well, that's not very helpful either," Tom said.

"I know." Something was working away in my brain. "But what if we *planned* something unexpected?"

Leese blinked in incredulity.

"You know, make something look like it's just random. When it's not. Then Mrs. Phillips will react suddenly to try to take advantage of the circumstances. She'll just… fall in."

"But we'll know that's what she'll do," Leese thought out loud, "and we'll plan for her to act like that."

"Exactly. We'll *anticipate* what looks like something random."

"But then it's not random," Tom exclaimed with a provoking grin.

"*That's* not helpful," Leese said, slightly annoyed.

CHAPTER EIGHTEEN

The next day was brutal. Everyone sensed the anger and frustration of Mrs. Phillips, but it was reserved particularly for me. I was beginning to feel a little embarrassed that all my classmates were suffering because of me even if they were unaware of its cause. Occasionally, a classmate would look at me with pity or raise an eyebrow as if to say, "What's going on?" Leese attempted several times to distract Mrs. Phillips by showing special interest in a subject, and with some success. The fire of wrath had not entirely consumed the roots of her teaching vocation which lay uncharred, hidden still beneath the wreckage of her classroom. But there remained, despite all attempts, a relentless assault on us all, veiled as a war against our untutored and resistant minds. There are many ways to wreak revenge, I learned. Snap quizzes, questions asked with a hint of contempt, sneers and ironic comments that leave no doubt about the abyss of one's general ignorance.

Tom, alone, was uncowed, but even he was fast using up his unearned bank of goodwill. Gone was the arbitrary indulgence he had taken for granted, and he relapsed, like the rest of us, into a resigned silence.

It dawned on me that, despite her seemingly flawless organization, Mrs. Phillips' dictatorial style actually revealed a caprice that played favourites wherever it would, and that now, with the same arbitrariness, it played inquisitor. It was the mere relaxation of her exigencies here, and the sudden rigidity of them there, that allowed her to govern in her little realm. A balance was maintained by a judicious, if unconscious, relenting or stiffening of her method.

But what would happen if we did not respond in kind? What if, instead of organizing our day so that Mrs. Phillips would not single us out, we deliberately acted against her anticipated reactions? It was time for a calculated experiment. I rose from my seat to fetch a pen from my shelf at the back. Leese glanced my way until she caught my eye.

I wasn't even out of my seat before a sharp rebuke was hurled my way. I ignored it. "I just need to get a pen…" and I continued. The usual castigation for not anticipating my needs *before* the period began was delivered with unusual vehemence. I said nothing and simply completed my action. I could feel Mrs. Phillips glowering at me, but I ignored it and began testing the pen on the corner of my school workbook, not looking up or even around the classroom.

I waited exactly ten minutes and then got up again, this time to fetch some paper. Mrs. Phillips seemed to vibrate with indignation, and her right hand shook ever so slightly. She shouted with a piercing shriek, "Sit down!"

"Just need some paper…." And after I got it, I sat down, as commanded. I did not look at her as I commenced testing my pen again on the blank page.

Seething with wrath, she ordered me to go to the principal's office to report my behaviour.

"For getting a piece of paper?" I mildly inquired, although my heart was racing so fast I thought my temples would burst. I remained sitting, my face innocent with an inquiring look.

Perceiving her rout, she turned purple with silence, her mouth open. There was no turning back now. The whole room froze, awaiting the unknown, petrified with anticipation of they knew not what.

But I had chosen my moment well. The bell startled everyone, and Mrs. Phillips seemed to shake out of some trance. She wordlessly left the room and her students — now released from her invisible hold — and strode towards lunch.

Anger is a powerful motive, but it is faceless. It seizes hold and blinds. Wrath transforms one into something one is not. There is no remedy once it possesses its victim. The only remedy is anticipation, to prepare in advance and remove the trigger that will set it in motion. The only defence against anger is to ambush it before it grabs hold.

Despite the cold and the wind, Tom, Leese, and I went out after gobbling our lunch in haste and silence. A damper had been thrown over us after the morning's excoriating performance.

"What were you doing?" Tom finally asked when we were out of earshot.

"I was trying something."

"Well, it didn't work."

But, actually, I knew it had.

"You provoked her," Leese said. "She won't like you for that."

"I don't think she'll like me anyway." Tom shrugged his shoulders as if to agree. "Anyway, I'm not sure it's about liking me or not liking me. She's frustrated that her plan has been taken away from her. Well, the plan she had once she'd taken my stamp."

"It's like it just fell into her lap, and now it's been stolen from her," Leese said. "It's probably worse because she didn't expect to suddenly get something so valuable. It's like a shortcut to getting rich, and then it's suddenly taken away. It makes you mad."

But the same thing had happened to me and I wasn't mad. I had been incredulous and shocked. But I wasn't exactly angry. I had felt I was betrayed. And I had felt I was letting my ancestor down.

We walked to the perimeter of the school playing field. The school was located at the very edge of the suburbs. Across the street were the old railway tracks leading into the city. They had been abandoned some years ago when all the local houses were built and the trains had been rerouted to a less obstructive path through the expanding city. We could not really see the tracks because they were hidden behind a sound barrier erected in the days when the suburbs were expanding but not yet built right up to the side rail. The barrier was a great, ugly wall of horizontal concrete rails piled one on top of the other and slotted into long channels of upright posts. The stark fence was about ten metres high, screening the diesel motors and the railcars that had fueled behind it. At irregular interstices, openings were left in the wall, high enough and wide enough for a human to pass through. Most were now boarded up, and a few were closed with a wire mesh that allowed us to peer through. Abandoned railcars could be seen through the wire screen, rusting under the pale winter sky. One or two openings retained an industrial turnstile hinged at the centre of the opening. No doubt they were left so that no one would find themselves utterly trapped in the railyard.

The three of us had walked along the enormous wall many times. When standing next to it the sounds of the schoolyard echoed down the length of the barrier, reflecting the noise and creating the odd sensation of eavesdropping on the conversations, even though those speaking stood at a distance that normally would make the shouts of children indiscernible.

We were not allowed out of the school ground during lunchtime, but events of the morning had so taken us out of our habits that we found ourselves walking next to the towering barrier. The crunch of snow underfoot dampened all sound as we escaped from the frenzied play of the children and the din of their shrieks and shouts. We were walking in silence when behind us we could discern hurried footsteps in the snow. I felt the hair on the back of my head stand up and the blood in my veins turn to ice. We all three turned at once to see Mrs. Phillips pursuing us. She wore no coat despite the wind and winter cold. Her face was chilled and set into a manic and intensely focused stare upon us. Behind her, clearly in better possession of her wits, was the elegant but none too happy Mrs. Lina Feher — Lana White — alternately walking and trotting in the snow, trying to keep pace with Mrs. Phillips. The school ground seemed far away and no one noticed us.

Mrs. Phillips said nothing, but the sheer determination on her face shouted warning. I must have triggered some unpredictable reaction that now took over. All three of us began to run forward. "She's snapped," was all Tom said.

"And she's gaining on us!" Leese cried out.

Impossible as it seemed, it was true. We were slipping in the snow with heavy boots. We passed one of the screened openings and I glimpsed a few scattered and empty railway cars. Tom was out in the lead and he stopped abruptly at a rusty turnstile. He pushed but it would not move.

"Quickly," he said and beckoned us up to the opening. He clasped his two hands together and lowered them close to the ground. Leese stepped into the human sling and Tom propelled her up and through the opening above the turnstile. It was narrow, but she slid easily through. Then he beckoned to me and I tried, but my size made it difficult and slow. "Hurry," Tom yelled, a slight panic in his voice. I squeezed through and then he followed, somehow leaping over the stile and throwing himself onto the ground inside the railyard.

All was silent except for the wind that blew along the tall fence. Small snow cyclones twirled along the great sound barrier as the wind caught at the concrete structure and was trapped.

Tom leapt up and looked wildly around. He started off towards one of the abandoned cars not too far distant. I'm not sure what his plan was. The car was located along the sound barrier. He scurried up the old ladder that formed part of the railway car, allowing maintenance persons to climb onto the roof. We all reached the top and now we could see farther, but the wall was higher than the car and we could not see over it. From our vantage point, we could see the breadth of the railyard. In fact, it was not all that wide: the space of about five rail lines. On the far side a low chain link fence was bent from people trying to climb over into the yard. Dismal industrial sheds and unpainted metal buildings lined the length of the chain link fence, disused and dilapidated. We could hear Mrs. Feher calling out to Mrs. Phillips now at the turnstile entrance. Looking down, our footsteps in the snow left a clear betrayal of our location. Tom clambered down and waited for us. "We have to get to the far side and over the fence." There seemed no other plan, but waiting for rescue on the roof of the railway car seemed ridiculous. Mrs. Phillips was clearly not interested in a game of "king of the castle." She wanted a black queen, and she was determined to get it.

Once down, we sped off to the chain link fence and as I turned, I could see Mrs. Phillips very unceremoniously squeezing through the opening. Mrs. Feher was remonstrating with her in her clipped accent, "But no.

NO! This will not do! What are we doing? Calm down, Mrs. Phillips. This won't get you anywhere." But Mrs. Phillips popped through and Mrs. Feher had no choice but to follow.

We managed to get to the fence and hopped over it with relative ease. Then we sped past the abandoned buildings which hunkered down against the winter sky, providing the only obstacles to the wind that raced off the prairie. Even if she could not see us, our snow prints would tell her where we were. There was no option but to run, to out-run our teacher.

Which should have been easy.

We came to a dismal street, long abandoned when the railway fell into disuse. The snow reflected the pale sky making it quite bright in the lowering afternoon sun. But brightness did not bring warmth. The snow cast a freshness to the scene, but abandoned piles of rubble, faded painted business signs, and scars of rusting metal machinery peeked through the whitewashed scene, hinting at a depressing graveyard of industrial detritus.

Leese looked up the length of the street, then back down, wondering which way to go. Tom stood still, paralyzed by the cold silence.

"Back towards the school," was all Leese said, and started running. None of us was sure how to find our way back to the playground. We had never paid much attention to the formidable sound barrier and we did not know how long it extended down the road that ran parallel to the school, or whether there was any unshuttered opening through which to find our way back.

I could hear the faint din of traffic ahead and hoped that spilling out onto a busy roadway would save us from an unhinged Mrs. Phillips. We ran towards the noise. I glanced back, and Mrs. Phillips was a small but manic figure following us. Mrs. Feher seemed to have left Mrs. Phillips to her plight and I could not see her. I had no clear idea what Mrs. Phillips would do if she managed to catch us. So far, we were increasing our distance, although slowly. We had the disadvantage of scouting our way forward through unknown territory, when all she had to do was keep her eyes forward on us to know a direct path to the object of her pursuit. There was the danger that in turning to the right or to the left we would find ourselves at a dead end, trapped between a high barrier we could never hope to scale and the menacing and unpredictable attack of a person who had locked away all caution in a classroom now empty.

Tom suddenly pointed ahead and to the left, and when I caught up to where he was, I could see what he intended. The road curved slowly and then abruptly ended just as the railway line continued along an overpass. The wide roadway intersecting the railway's path disappeared under the tracks and the tall barrier ended at the beginning of the overpass. A large warehouse fronted the road along the curve, a last industrial access to the freighted goods pulled by rail transport. Tom and Leese were heading to the end of the road, intending to escape at the very spot where the wall ended and the overpass began. Another chain link fence abutted against the concrete slabs out of which the barrier was constructed, but it was pulled back and in disrepair, providing a narrow gate of passage. Glancing back, I could see we were out of the line of sight of Mrs. Phillips, having just rounded the curve in the street.

I suddenly tripped on some solid metal object and tumbled to the ground. As I jumped up, my right leg buckled under me and I could see the trouser leg torn and a gash opened along my leg. In my panic, I suppressed the pain and wrestled to get up. Tom and Leese turned back to me, but I waved them forward. My thoughts strangely coalesced and from panic my mind turned to clarity. "Go on!" I yelled, "I'll be right there. I'm okay." I was not okay, as a matter of fact, but I had made a deliberate choice. Mrs. Phillips' anger was directed at me, not at Tom and Leese. I, Ivan the Giant, would confront it alone. The decision was sudden and very clear. I was unsteady, but I could move. It felt like I was dragging my legs that would not completely obey my command. The warehouse that I had fallen beside lay large and obstructive. It was boarded up, but I noticed a slight sway to the door and I instantly moved towards it. The snow-covered metal pile I had tripped on was a forgotten remnant of that industrial complex, abandoned by the roadside.

The door was stuck and for a moment I thought it would not give, so I gave it a shove with my shoulder, as my leg was useless to kick it in. It gave way easily, rusting hinges groaning under my weight. I tumbled onto the concrete floor that was cold, hard, and covered with dirt and sand. A thin film of snow covered the floor at the door, forced in by the wind blowing through the gaps. All else was dark, in contrast to the pale sky outside, and I could make out no discernable trace of wall or room. I lay for a moment and then shoved my hands under my hips and leveraged my way onto my feet. I pushed the door shut. The curious smell of smoke lingered over the remnant odours of grease and unwashed bodies. This must be a refuge for those who passed their lives on the streets. An unguarded shelter. I heard no human voice now. As my eyes adjusted to the dim interior, I could see that the outdoor light seeped into the building at random cracks in the ceiling or walls that had been left to fall to ruin against the onslaught of the harsh elements. The building formed one gigantic space sectioned off by great square concrete pillars that stretched overhead to the rafters high above. This was a cavernous space designed for gigantic machinery that no longer filled its void. A slight flap of wings sounded distant, like an echo over a great ravine. Where to go? Mrs. Phillips would see my path through the snow, but also the path of Tom and Leese to the breach in the wall. Which would she follow? Where to hide in this enormous cavern?

> *One fish*
> *Two fish*
> *Red fish*
> *Blue fish.*

Hide in plain sight. At least in here there were no footprints in the snow. If she entered, I would have the advantage for a moment before her eyes adjusted. I limped over to a near pillar not far from the door where I could see her enter. She would expect me to run to a darkened, recessed corner to hide, but I would stay by the door. With any luck she would walk past me before her eyes adjusted to the forbidding darkness.

I heard a heavy breath and a tentative push on the door. The rusty hinges groaned but did not yield. Following a moment of reflection and an intake of breath, a violent kick sent the reluctant door screaming and slamming against the wall. A small, menacing figure peered inside and stepped over the threshold.

CHAPTER NINETEEN

M rs. Phillips could not see deep within until her eyes adjusted to the dark. She squinted and strained her neck forward, then began to move while deliberately keeping her gaze straight ahead. Clearly, she assumed that whoever had entered would seek out the back recesses of the building and the security of yet deeper spaces. My calculation had been right in that respect, anyway. The door lay open, but little light penetrated into the great hall of the warehouse. In times past it may have been used to store wares that were delivered off the railcars. My eyes had adjusted to the dim, and it seemed now that perhaps it wasn't a warehouse at all, but a repair depot for enormous machinery. The floor was roughly poured concrete and the heavy petrol odour seeped from it.

The logical thing to do would have been to run to the open door, but for some unthought reason I remained where I was, brushed up against a pillar. I could slip around it silently out of the line of sight of Mrs. Phillips. She was halfway down the space and had halted. I could see her head cast a glance to the right and to the left and then tilt to take in the full height of the open iron rafters that held the roof together. She did not think to look behind her. She suddenly pulled her shoulders up and her back rigid, standing absolutely still as if straining to hear the sounds that would reveal my location. The sudden flapping of wings overhead released her from the trance and she exhaled very loudly. Did she think I was in? She had followed my path in the snow rather than the path of Tom and Leese. My footprints were larger than theirs.

"Ivan!" she called in a voice that throttled against the void. The syllables fell idle as soon as they were pronounced and gave place to no echo. The great space swallowed it whole. "Ivan!" she repeated, at a slightly higher pitch that resonated more clearly but still died as suddenly as it was spoken. She emitted an exasperated clicking of her tongue that I knew well from the classroom. A vigorous action would follow after a brief pause. She spun 180 degrees and took in the whole expanse of the industrial tomb, squinting again in my direction before spinning round to search out the far wall of the building. I felt myself freeze automatically but I controlled any quick intake of breath. I made myself appear in shadow as a part of the concrete pillar. Again, I knew the logical thing would be to run to the door but I remained in my place. It was very likely she could outrun me, with the gash on my leg now hindering my free movement. Then again, I was at least as tall as she. But how many action stories I had read described people accomplishing feats beyond their strength when under the influence of fear or rage or desperation? Which was the passion that now drove her into this gigantic shed to seek me out? What could she hope to accomplish by confronting me?

In that moment, very suddenly, the way forward seemed revealed before me with singular clarity.

She would not confront me. I would confront her.

"Yes," I said. The monosyllable stuck in the back of my throat with a hoarseness that could only have been heard in that great stillness. Wings surged overhead again, with a swoosh in the darkened air. Mrs. Phillips pivoted round to my direction, but she could not see me.

"Ivan?" she almost whispered back.

"What are you doing, Mrs. Phillips?"

Silence.

"What?"

A pause.

"What are you doing? Why are you here?" I asked. It was well and truly a question she could have put to me, but she seemed not to reflect. She continued to look about, trying to fix her dimmed sight on me, but could not find me, hiding in plain view like a giant pillar.

It was very strange. "Where's your coat?" I asked. It was a question without context. It was she who looked to see that her students were properly dressed. She shivered and looked down at herself, realizing for the first time, it seemed, that the winter cold was a threat. The question threw her off balance.

"My coat?"

Mrs. Phillips was someone who thrived on predictability and foresight, the foundations of order and control. Now she was disrobed of self-mastery. Instinctively, I knew she would fall into one pattern or another. Either she would cloak her volatility again into the folds of her outer reserve, or she would release it full-blown and without restraint upon me. I waited to see which it would be.

"Ivan!" she shouted, startling me. My weak leg buckled for a moment and I had to shift my weight suddenly with a scraping of my foot on loose debris, a brusque reaction that revealed my open disguise. She locked her gaze on me and set herself in great strides to meet me. I tested my leg. It was not strong and I knew it would not hold out for long. But she did not know that and it was best not to let her see. Wounded prey stands little chance against a savage aggressor that attacks directly at any weakness. I stood my ground but calculated the trajectory of flight to the open door in case it should become necessary. I could have used some of Captain America's tactical strategy at this point, but at least my inelegant lunges across the basketball court may, after all, have provided some practice to serve for my rescue.

I could hear the faint shuffle of dust and gravel beneath her feet, so clear and cold the air was. The flutter of wings was suspended overhead and no sounds from outside penetrated into the recesses of this old warehouse. Mrs. Phillips halted abruptly a pace in front of me, pulling herself up as if from the last vestiges of some automatic internal restraint. My eyes were even with her forehead, and it was the first time I knew for certain that I was taller than she, if only just. The furrows in that forehead worked from a mechanism within.

Suddenly, without any hint or anticipation, the internal restraint failed and her arms bolted out, hands open in claws. But they stopped just before they reached me and then withdrew, her hands falling suddenly limp by her side. It was not hatred I read in the lines of her face and the flash of her eyes; it was something else I could not then name. Later I would understand. It was despair, the poisoned fruit of hatred, hatred that had burned itself out leaving only the embers of desperation and the dying coals of dreams and illusions.

I did not even see it happen. I was suddenly knocked onto my back and my head hit the concrete. I lay dazed. I had fainted once from heat and the sensation was the same, the feeling of having lost a few precious seconds of life that could never be recovered. They were lost between the shock of blacking out and the disoriented state of recovery. Mrs. Phillips didn't approach me in those seconds but stood where she was, looking down at me but not looking at me. She had built a fortress fashioned from the structure of rules and order which had long provided her with the illusion of solidity. But within, at the heart, was no treasure to be guarded, only an emptiness to be hidden. Her world could exist with certainty only within the finitude of a classroom, and when the void was finally brought into the open air, the frailty of its structure was revealed. It collapsed. The illusion now burst.

Lying on the ground, now alert, I felt no rush of fear, strangely. Perhaps it was knowing that I was taller and at least as strong as she. But really, it was something else. Her own fear completely filled the empty space and left none for me. Not a fear of me, exactly. A fear of having lost her way. Nor did I feel anger at her brutality, only a sadness.

My life, in its own way, had been empty, filled only with the life given it by others, breathed into it by parents and teachers. That was at an end. Mrs. Phillips had no life left to breathe into me.

I struggled to get up, but my leg would not support me and my head spun. Mrs. Phillips stood and watched me, as she would an insect in her garden.

"I almost had it, you know," she whispered.

I stared at her for a moment. "Almost."

"You wouldn't have missed it."

I wasn't so sure, but I let her satisfy her own need for justification.

"My great-grandfather hid her for me to find."

No understanding registered in the brow of her forehead. Incomprehension. Maybe it was silly of me to think I had some loyalty to a long-deceased ancestor who had never known me. Still, family must count for something in the bigger scheme of things.

We seemed lost in the vast empty warehouse, with me lying on the ground, she bearing over me. Ivan the Giant had never been my identity. Giant compared to what? I hated the nickname. Always had.

Silence ensued. Then the flash and swoosh of wings.

Mrs. Phillips was pulling herself back. She slapped her hands together, aware now of the dust on them. She arched her neck and took in the great space around us, wondering, it seemed, how she found herself there, by what powers of locomotion she had been brought here. She looked at me again, staring at me as from a great distance.

It was then that the rush of voices entered through the opened door that had been slammed back when Mrs. Phillips entered. Tom, Leese, Principal Marjonson, Mr. Carruthers, and Walter. Walter came right up to me and examined my leg with a summary view. He said nothing, but reached down and drew me up in one movement. I needed his strength, as I could not yet stand on my own. He brushed the hair from my forehead with a graceful and tender touch, just as he must have done when I was an infant. I was, after all, still his child.

Mr. Carruthers confronted Mrs. Phillips and they were in some wordless battle now, staring each other down. As Mr. Carruthers had the stronger part, and as Mrs. Phillips knew it, there was not much to say, but only a show of mutual disapproval. He looked back at me and asked, "How did you fall, Ivan?"

"I must have tripped," was all I said. I didn't look up. No sense making things worse. I *had* tripped. Outside. It wasn't a lie, exactly.

My father just looked into my eyes, reading something there. After a moment, he nodded. "All right."

Mr. Carruthers looked doubtful but kept his peace.

Tom and Leese held back. The principal had a rather complex look on his face, as if he were in trouble but had just escaped imminent danger in some inexplicable way. Which, I suppose, he had. Teachers knocking students around would complicate his afternoon.

I began to shiver and Tom took off his coat, wrapping it around me. "Best to keep the wounded warm," was all he said. He shivered beside Leese, who looked proudly at him as if he had just performed an act of gallant chivalry. This was something she could appreciate.

EPILOGUE

———◆►◄◆———

Mrs. Phillips did not show up for class the next day, or any day after that. A new teacher appeared, Mrs. Joly, which she pronounced after the French manner with all soft consonants and long vowels. She spoke with just the trace of an accent, which made her somewhat exotic, aside from the fact that she had the blondest hair I had ever seen.

Mrs. Joly was kindly, but she was stepping into a post without any preparation. Mrs. Phillips would have pursed her lips in disapproval. But then again, Mrs. Phillips was the cause of Mrs. Joly's predicament. Contrary to the movies you see or the books you read, we did not give Mrs. Joly a hard time or take advantage of her awkward situation. Tom lost his privileges without complaint and started to show up on time, even a little early. Leese continued as usual, which, in itself, was to be expected. She was a self-contained little person. She had no charm with which to charm a new teacher, but over time she would become appreciated. She knew she had to wait.

There was somewhat less order and discipline within the walls of the classroom, but no one seemed to mind. The work got done. At the front of the room, Mrs. Joly did not lock her desk or stick to any rigid system of organization. Flexibility seemed to be her rule. She could ebb and flow with the hours of the day, and time was her friend, not her enemy.

Basketball season ended and I did not join any other teams. Sports would not be my thing. I wasn't sure what exactly "my thing" would be, but not that. I felt, too, that time would be needed to sort it all out. Tom figured out that he would become a biologist and he started spending more time after school helping Mr. Maugher in the science room, cleaning fish tanks or cleaning the cages of almost-domesticated rodents. Leese and I helped him sometimes. But Leese would see her way forward through history. Not "social sciences" as the course was called, but proper history. People who made lousy decisions or good decisions, for good reasons or for bad, with consequences beyond their own limited vision. The realm not of kings or ambition, but of human beings making a mess of things and then trying to sort it out. Foolishness and wisdom indifferently played out over the course of a life.

The half hour reserved for hobbies — avocations, as Mr. Carruthers would call them — was not continued by Mrs. Joly. No one felt they suffered for the want of it. Hobbies are fickle things, and none more so than for eleven-year-olds. Still, it had served its purpose. Serious play had taught me many things I should not have otherwise learned, or perhaps learned so quickly. Stern monarchs from distant times still influence the lives of their subjects in peculiar and unexpected ways. Greed can veil the emptiness of fear or inarticulate ambition. Even the most applied of minds can act on caprice and take uncalculated risk. In a strange way, Mrs. Phillips had become more human to me — not because I pitied her or resented her or feared her, but perhaps because I began to know her as I had begun to know myself. Once in a while I would take a detour by her house. She had not moved away or disappeared from the neighbourhood. She planted an orderly garden, clipped her lawn in a regular pattern, and continued to meet up with people for lunch or to play the violin. She had a life. She had hobbies. I hadn't robbed her of those.

Nor had she robbed me of mine.

Mr. Carruthers returned to the dust of his shop, and I would go from time to time as I grew. My interest in philately grew as well, and he continued to mentor me in ways he did not know. My vocabulary increased in his presence and I developed an appreciation for detail. It is in the details, after all, that our differences are revealed and brought to value. Friendship flourishes in the richness of our differences, in the joy we feel when someone has what we do not possess or shares with us what we could never claim as our own.

Walter and Macy continued to structure my days with a benign regency until the day came when I would structure my own. I did not transform into a rebellious son, although I had my own mind which I did not yet always know. We drew closer in a quiet sort of way. My growth spurt ended as abruptly as it had started, and eventually my classmates stopped calling me Ivan the Giant. I was fine with that. Relieved, in fact. Undeserved notoriety is a burden. Maybe deserved notoriety is too, for all I know.

I held on to my Penny Black. My stern queen remained safely stored. She would be of use to me at some future time, I was sure, just as she had been trouble for me in the past. I felt grateful to my distant and ancestral father who had trusted me with her safekeeping, and I felt that I had honoured his trust. So, as they say, at least there was that.

Made in the USA
San Bernardino, CA
09 November 2019